HELL-BENT GENTS

Clay Mandell helps the sheriff of Waco to keep the lid on the lawless town. Waco has plenty of hell-bent gents, and the leading guy is Rolf Lester, brother of Mary, the girl Clay so admires. Fights and escapes from death are destined to confront Clay — and so is Rolf, who is planning robberies on the railroad and the mining camps. Mary's brother is using her ranch as a headquarters for various ruffians, so Clay finds himself caught between his duty as a lawman and his love for the girl.

JOHN BLAZE

HELL-BENT GENTS

Complete and Unabridged

LINFORD
Leicester

First published in Great Britain in 1990 by
Robert Hale Limited
London

Robert Hale Limited
London

British Library CIP Data

Blaze, John
Hell-bent gents.—Large print ed.—
Linford western library
I. Title II. Series
823.914 [F]

ISBN 0–7089–7489–9

269p 19cm

Published by
F. A. Thorpe (Publishing) Ltd.
Anstey, Leicestershire

Set by Words & Graphics Ltd.
Anstey, Leicestershire
Printed and bound in Great Britain by
T. J. Press (Padstow) Ltd., Padstow, Cornwall

This book is printed on acid-free paper

1

HE came up out of the arid desert, a tall grim young man stooped on a horse equally as bone-tired as himself. His Stetson was yellow with dust and his red bandana hung around his neck like a sweat-stained rag. On the left side of his flannel shirt was a tarnished star with the legend 'Deputy' engraved on it.

Behind him was another horse, on a rope, a led animal with dust and horse-sweat mixed. In this silent wasteland where only distant vultures wheeled in the sky, they made a strange trio.

Clay Mandell licked his dry lips, wished he could drink, but knew his water bottle had long since gone dry. Staring into the heat haze, he could see the distant township of Waco. The lawless town in this neck of Texas was no mirage, for which he thanked God.

He was almost back home after his three day and almost non-stop ride into the badlands.

He settled back into the saddle, resting one arm on the horn. Tired and grim, full of morose thoughts about the results of his trip, he was content to let the horse take him into Waco.

Without the dusty stubble of beard, Clay Mandell was a good-looking, slow-smiling guy with a strong sense of justice — and that had prompted him to take on the job of deputy sheriff. He had some good ideas about maintaining law and order and some day, when he had graduated to the position of sheriff, he wanted to put these theories into full practice. With Waco booming under the combined influence of cattle and railroad construction, the job of a lawman was not an easy one.

He was met three miles out of the town by a party of four men who were riding across the dry grassland with a thunder of hoofs. On sighting Clay Mandell they reined in at a wave from

2

one of the men, and waited until the tired horse plodded along the trail.

"Howdy Clay," greeted the bulky man with the bristling red moustache. He jerked hard eyes at the weary led horse and its empty saddle. "So you got him?"

"I got him, Sheriff," assented Clay grimly. There was a complete lack of humour in his voice. "I got Tad Lester. He waited for me with a rifle but I stalked around him and got him. He's buried now. I piled the stones over him."

"So you brought his horse back as proof," returned Sheriff Hoot Sampson. "Good for you, Clay. Reckon that'll show some of the hard guys in this town that murder ain't no laughing business — which is what too many of 'em think it is. Reckon young Rolf Lester might quit riding herd with them gun-toting idiots who are just spoiling for a fight most of the time."

Clay nodded tiredly. He had only one nagging thought, and that was:

What would Mary Lester think of him when she learned he had killed her elder brother, Tad?

Tad Lester, a red-blooded young fool with a low-slung Colt, had gone too far. He had shot up a railroad office one night. All might have gone well for the rannigan had not a daring clerk grabbed at his mask — and got lead slugs for his pains — as his identity was revealed. The clerk had lived to tell the tale. But another man was dead. Tad had ridden out, obviously for the border, through the badlands. And Clay had gone out after him only some hours later, following the man's track with the aid of a bright moon. It had been a long ride into the desert country, away from the Texas grasslands, with the trail-wise Tad trying all his tricks to shake off a lone pursuer. But the end had come in Colt smoke after three days in the saddle.

"Wal, get yourself some shut-eye, Clay," advised Hoot Sampson. "And don't worry none. Reckon everything will work out fine in the end."

He was trying to be kind in his rough fashion. Sheriff Hoot Sampson knew Clay had called on Mary Lester more than a few times, in spite of her two gun-happy brothers. Mary and her brothers ran the Circle Four ranch, raising Texas Longhorns on the range. Their father had died like Tad, in a gun-fight with the law. Mary, too, was a trifle wild — but fascinatingly pretty.

"We were on our way to the railroad," said the sheriff. "Been another derailment and a payroll stolen. Damn these owl-hoots! A man can't rest for long in this town. I reckon I earn my dinero."

The three other men, who evidently made a posse, laughed loudly at this remark. Then the four riders turned their big sleek horses and thundered away down the sparsely grassed valley.

Clay touched spur to his tired bay and the horse plodded on again. He himself sank low in the saddle, thinking of Mary Lester. His thoughts were now a turmoil because it was pretty sure that the girl would hate him. What else? Just when he was getting to know her nicely, this had to happen.

He reached the streets of Waco and came down the main stem to the sheriff's office. He took the two animals into the stable at the back of the brick-built building and handed them over to the livery man. He walked around to the front again, stolidly, thinking of the dead man out in the wasteland, then using a key he let himself into the office.

He passed Hoot Sampson's quarters. The sheriff was an unmarried man, his mode of living having fashioned him that way. Clay, too, had a room on the second floor. Often he wondered if his life might turn out to be like that of Hoot Sampson, a man without a woman in his life because of the job. After meeting Mary, he had hoped not — but maybe if she began to hate him that would be his destiny.

At the back of the substantial building was a big office and a passage that led to four iron-barred stone-built cells. The place was empty right now. The bad and ugly of Waco seemed to prefer to die rather than be caught.

Clay washed and shaved, driving back the dead feeling to lie down and sleep for ever. Then he went to his room and changed, donning clean trousers of brown material and a blue gaberdine shirt which stretched tight across his chest. He got out a new fawn Stetson. He polished his boots slowly until the black leather was shining again, and he wiped off the specks of horse blood from his spurs. Feeling the need to get rid of the wastelands completely, he donned leather brass-studded cuffs on his wrists and then pulled out some riding gloves from a drawer. His last act was to fasten a new red neckerchief around his neck.

He went out to the stable, thinking he looked good even if he was bone tired. Good enough to call on Mary Lester, he hoped.

As he got to the boardwalk a brawny six-footer stepped forward and barred his way.

"Howdy, Rolf," drawled Clay Mandell.

He was Mary's brother, the brother of the dead man, Tad Lester!

The other's lips were a thin tight line. "You've killed Tad! I saw you ride in with his horse. By God, I nearly plugged you there and then, Mandell — but I don't reckon to swing for a stinking lousy law-man."

Rolf Lester threw his gunbelt to the boardwalk with a sudden clatter. He'd had the belt half-unfastened when he had barred Clay's path.

"Drop yours!" spat the big blond young buckeroo.

Clay smiled slowly, staring into the other man's bitter eyes. He began to slowly unbuckle his single gunbelt with the shiny leather holster, working deliberately, taking a lot of time over the simple operation. He smiled at the other guy, no anger, which was a contrast to Rolf Lester's weatherbeaten visage now contorted in a fury.

"Get that damned belt off! I don't aim to get shot in the back — which is what a stinking law-man would do! Why the slow play? You figure the sheriff will be here to back you up? I can tell you, Mandell, he's down at the railroad. Get your blamed hands up and start fightin'! I aim to beat you to a pulp!"

"You sure talk a lot," said Clay slowly.

He felt every tired muscle in his body tense for the forthcoming effort. This wasn't something he relished. He'd had little sleep in the past thirty-eight hours and little to eat in the way of red meat. He had intended to ride over at once to see Mary Lester and try to explain. But first he had to fight her brother. He had killed the other brother. Now he was being forced into fighting this young rannigan with the strength of a Brahma bull.

Clay's belt dropped. Old in experience of rough-house, he stepped back. Rolf's fist, which had lashed out fiercely as the gun-belt dropped, slashed thin air.

Clay summoned his tired strength and rammed a fist to the other's solar plexus. The bones in his arm jarred. It was like slamming rock. Then Rolf's left swung in a shuddering uppercut.

The gloved fist caught Clay before his slowed reaction could enable him to dodge. The hefty blow staggered him and he went backwards, falling from the edge of the boardwalk. In falling, he tripped and fell heavily in the dusty road. But he lurched up quickly enough to find Rolf swiftly on him.

Clay threw a hard left to Rolf's savage face, using all his flagging energy. But Rolf Lester was still fresh and rode the punch with a short sneering laugh that breathed contempt. His arms forked out in a fury but with the surge of a piston. Savage blows jerked Clay's head upwards, clouding his senses and making him reel. His hands became incapable of speedy reaction, feeling like lead. Clay's gloved fists tried to fend off Rolf Lester's red-blooded pounding. Clay fell back against a post supporting the upper storey of the wood office. And so Rolf Lester bored in and planted solid, relentless blows to his opponent's face.

The deputy sheriff slid slowly down the post, his mouth twisted as he sucked gasping breath. He crouched on the dirt. He avoided one blow and then began to haul himself to his feet, using two hands to grasp the post.

He was an easy target for a savage man. Rolf Lester was picking his blows, and as Clay turned from the support of the wood post the other smashed his fists into him. Clay swayed, eyes bleak as he tried to focus on the other guy. His fists moved out slowly and Rolf slammed them down with a curt laugh. He planted a terrible right to

Clay's chin and then watched him fall with an odd slowness to the earth.

Three or four hard-bitten rannigans had gathered to watch the free show. Not one of them lifted a hand to help the deputy.

Rolf Lester shuffled closer to the fallen man. His blue eyes were bright with hatred.

"You won't be so fast with a hog-leg when I'm done with you!" he grated.

Clay's arm was outstretched as he sprawled, dazed, motionless.

Rolf Lester lifted his booted foot.

"I'll break every bone in your hand!" he gloated.

His foot was about to stamp down savagely on Clay's gun-hand when a man who had pushed across the road walked through the small group of onlookers. "You can keep that foot up high right where it is, Lester, you bastard!"

Rolf Lester looked into a firmly held Colt. For a moment he hesitated, tempted to stamp on Clay's hand and to hell with the consequences. Then, his blue eyes full of sardonic hate, he stepped back, stared at the newcomer and the implacable Colt.

The man with the gun was Jesse Teed, a rancher of about forty years of age. He was a respected man around Waco and a friend of Clay Mandell.

The deputy stirred and rose laboriously while Rolf Lester grinned into Jesse Teed's gun. Clay dusted his clothes and took deep breaths, staring at his grinning enemy.

"You sure messed me up a bit, Rolf," he drawled. "Hope it makes you happy." He drew another deep breath and added: "But watch out, feller. I won't feel so dead-beat the next time."

"You can watch out, too, Mandell," rapped back the man. He picked up his gunbelt and then turned and strode across the road and went into a saloon. With graven faces the handful of hard cases who had watched the fight strolled off. The event had been just another brawl to them.

"If there was any damned law around here that in-bitten Lester feller ought to be in jail for assault," fumed Jesse Teed.

Clay managed a smile. "Forget it, Jesse. I reckon we can call it a personal matter between me and that guy."

The rancher changed the subject abruptly. "Did you get his brother? That what he's so sore about? I did hear something as I rode into town.

Clay nodded. "Yeah. I had to shoot Tad. What else can you do when a jasper is laying for you with a Winchester? I was sure lucky to scout around him before he plugged me."

Clay walked stiffly to the boardwalk. Jesse watched him shrewdly. "You look all done in. Reckon you ought to get some rest, amigo. So it's war between you and that Lester feller. I reckon you could beat him in a fist fight if you were fitter."

"Forget it, Jesse," muttered Clay. "I

reckon I just took a beating, like a man has to do every now an then. I've had little sleep or rest for a lot of hours — but that don't mean anything."

"Wal, watch out for yourself, Clay . . ."

"I'm still determined to see Mary Lester at the Circle Four."

With Jesse Teed shaking his head at this decision, Clay returned to the sheriff's office to wash the blood from his face and knock some of the dust out of his clothes.

Jesse Teed muttered: "Now there's a galoot who don't know when he's had enough!"

Some ten minutes later Clay was riding a fresh horse down the well used trail leading east out of Waco. The Circle Four ranch was small and not as rich in grass as some, stretching into the rocky hills many miles to the east. The boundaries of the ranch were a good hour's ride out of town, even when the horse was urged to the limit. The ranch buildings were first reached, with the rest of the spread a narrow neck of land going into the hills.

The steers often strayed into these lands in their search for grass, but cholla cactus and Joshua trees flourished in the more arid parts. And in the hot silence rattlers basked in rocky nooks.

He knew he was terribly tired and maybe acting the fool, but he wanted to see Mary and talk to her honestly before the story of his killing of Tad Lester reached her ears in all the distortion that only rumour can provide. He just wanted to talk, see her, watch her face — that was all. He could not rest until he had done that.

But he still knew she would hate him. But maybe in time she would understand.

With the wariness bred in him as a lawman, he left the trail as he approached the Circle Four buildings. He came through a rocky defile, slowly, letting the animal take it easy after the urgent ride. Grass tufted in nooks and crannies, seemingly sparse but full of nourishment for cattle who had to hunt for sustenance. He halted his mount to stare at the Circle Four ranch-house and barns. The spread was small by some standards. Mary and Rolf Lester employed only one hand. Maybe they would have to hire another now that Tad, who had been the elder brother, was dead.

Death was a sombre business, Clay thought bitterly. While hunting down his man there had been only one thought and that was survival. Gunplay had eliminated one man in the game. That was the way he'd seen it, but now he realised there was a human side. Tad Lester, although a hellion to others and bent on trouble with the law, was still her brother, someone she'd known since childhood. And now he, the guy who had been forced to shoot the hell-bent, had to see Mary and plead understanding.

The ranch-house was silent with smoke rising from a chimney. Maybe Mary was cooking, for the day was too warm to need a fire. He could see a few horses in a corral, and the colourful little flower bed Mary had fashioned to brighten the front of the house. Of the girl there was no sign.

He was about to jig his horse forward again when he saw a buck-board rattle around the big cottonwoods and rush through the open gates of the ranch-yard.

Clay halted his mount and narrowed his eyes as he stared into the sun.

Mary Lester came to the ranch-house door, wiping her hands on her apron. Even the sight of her sent a strange longing through him. He wanted to ride up furiously and take her into his arms and comfort her. She'd need some comfort. He really wanted to tell the girl that he loved her. So far he had not talked like that. In that respect he was a taciturn man.

Instead of this human need for her, there was this watching game, the need to be wary because she had brothers with no respect for the law — except now that one was dead. And Clay felt a bit tired of this wariness that had been bred in him.

Clay thought that the man who drove the buck-board was Seth Mundy, the ranch-hand. He was about to ride forward when he saw Mundy grab at a box on the buck-board and carry the weighty thing into the ranch-house. The man swiftly returned for another. Although fairly small the boxes were a pretty weight, rectangular in shape. It dawned on Clay that he had seen long carpenter-made boxes like this before — at a bank.

Clay waited, puzzled. He saw Seth Mundy unload four of the boxes and carry them into the ranch-house. Clay felt grim, a nagging suspicion now in his mind that this was a bad business.

It came to him now. He'd seen rectangular boxes like this in use at gold mines and banks. They were lined with tin-plate and usually held gold dust and nuggets and were used by assayers. The gold was carried like

19

this, bags of small nuggets and dust inside until they could be melted into ingots.

What was Seth Mundy doing with these boxes?

Maybe they were old containers, bought cheap at a sale and used to carry something heavy. With sombre feelings, because deep down he had a hunch something was wrong, Clay Mandell waited. He hung around until the buck-board was unloaded and the horses unhitched. He saw the man take the buck-board around to the stables at the back of the house. Only then did Clay ride forward.

He came down slowly and rode into the ranch-yard, unsmiling, knowing that his initial task was now worsened. He hitched his horse's reins to a fence and walked up to the front porch.

Even before he got that far Mary Lester had seen him and she came slowly to see him. He saw fear in her blue eyes. He saw her smooth down her cherry-red gingham dress. She had fine features with generous lips, but there was this fear on her face right now. Her honey-coloured hair fell in waves at the back of her neck.

"Mary — I want — " he began.

Seth Mundy came out of the bunkhouse. He had heard the sound of the horse's hoofs and the voice.

"Howdy, deputy. Lookin' for some-body, mebbe?"

There was a curious note in the ranch-hand's voice. He was a lean waddy of indeterminate age, badly needing a shave — or maybe he never shaved except when he went to town. His hands were black with dirt and his clothes equally in the same condition. Clay shot a glance at this unpromising specimen, wondering how Mary put up with him around the place. He noted the man's hand was near his gun. He wondered why a cowboy should wear a gun while working. Many did not.

"Just hankering to talk with Miss Mary, feller," drawled Clay.

Seth Mundy's eyelids dropped as

if he was searching for significance behind the innocuous answer. He did not move away.

"Can I talk to you, Mary — inside?" asked Clay quietly.

She nodded as if lost for words. "Tad didn't mean to kill . . . Where is he — do you know? He got away, didn't he?" she stammered.

He came up beside her on the porch. His hand fell lightly on her sleeve and she glanced at him swiftly, wondering, questioning.

"They are just a bit wild, you know — Tad and Rolf," she said with an attempt at defiance. "But you don't understand that, do you?"

"Mary — Tad did not get away . . . "

She drew back and her blue eyes leaped to a brilliance full of fear. "What do you mean? You captured him?"

"No . . . "

"What has happened?"

"I had to shoot him," he said harshly. "It was him or me. He was pot-shooting at me with a rifle. He wanted to kill me because I was the law. I scouted around him — and had to shoot. A slug got him in the heart. Now you know, Mary — and I'm sure sorry."

She just stared at him, her cheeks going pale under her tan.

"Look, Mary, you've got to understand," said Clay urgently. "I was forced into the shootin'. I'm deputy sheriff. Tad killed a man. Maybe it was better for him to go out shooting than a — a rope — because that would have been his end."

"You did that — to *Tad*!"

"Mary, I wanted to come here and tell you about it myself afore the rumours get around. It was a fair fight — me or him! Mary, I want to help you . . . "

"You want to help me!" she flashed. "You killed my brother and then try to talk me over! There's nothing you can say now, Clay Mandell, that can make matters right between you and me. Don't come around here any more."

"But, Mary — I do want to help."

"Rolf was right — he said you were just trying to get something on Tad and him! Get out of here — before I go for a shotgun."

"You heard, feller," snapped Seth Mundy, and his hand fell to his gunbelt.

"I wouldn't if I were you," Clay jerked. His hand, too, fell near his gun.

Clay paused, at a loss for further words. He just wanted to touch her, console her, but with this damned rannigan, Mundy, near to hand this attempt at friendship was difficult. The inevitable had happened. His courting of the girl had crashed because of the troubles with her hellion brothers.

Clay walked down the porch steps and went over to his horse. At that very moment the drum of a horse's hoofs was heard on the hard land. Seconds later Rolf Lester rode furiously into the ranch yard and dismounted in a swift agile leap, his animal blowing as if it had been ridden by the devil.

When he appeared from behind his horse, he had a gun in his hand and it pointed menacingly at Clay.

"I oughta kill you right now, lawman, bastard!"

Mary ran down towards them. She clutched at her brother's arm. She shook her head several times and then found words. "No! No, Rolf, you fool! They'd hang you!"

"They'd have to get me first."

"I said, no! Let him ride away."

Something in the girl's voice caused Rolf to hesitate, some intonation which made him turn his head. Then he gave a glance at Seth Mundy and that rough range rider gave a significant nod of his tousled head.

Clay felt tempted to ram a fist into Rolf Lester's face and to hell with the gun. Anger was raging in his heart because he couldn't reason with the girl and he couldn't deal with her toughie brother. So he got on his saddle, staring grimly. He took up the leathers and looked at Mary. "Remember, when you want help I'll be around. Just ask me. I'll do anything to help you, Mary: an' if you ask me you'll sure need it pretty soon."

"What in tarnation do you mean by that, lawman?" yelled Rolf Lester.

Clay could have mentioned the rectangular wood boxes that had gone into the house. But grimly, he jigged his horse around and headed out of the Circle Four ranch yard with complete indifference to the young buckeroo's gun.

He'd taken a chance. He seen that the fellow was full of drink. The young fool had been in a saloon before his violent ride to the ranch.

Out on the trail again, Clay just sank low in the saddle, tired and at a low ebb. Usually, he sat tall in the saddle, a proud riding man, but he was suddenly down at heart. Mary would hate him from now on. He had seen it in her eyes, a terrible gleam. The odds were all against their friendship turning into real love; and that was what he had hoped their path would take. He was ready to court her, love her, but everything was going against him.

He rode slowly towards Waco, fed up and physically tired. A man could be brought low by events other than bullets in the flesh.

When Clay got back to Waco and entered the sheriff's office, he found Hoot Sampson stamping around, full of bad temper, glowering at the window and smoking a long black cigar so furiously the office was filled with a fog.

"Howdy, Clay. Where you been?"

"Does it matter?" Clay was in a bad mood, too.

"Hell knows whether it will matter. You know something?"

"What?"

"That wasn't a payroll that was stolen from the derailed car. It was bullion — twelve thousand dollars of gold in them long boxes!"

Clay bunched his fists and felt momentarily helpless.

Because he had a shrewd idea where that gold was cached. But what the hell could he do about it? Anything he said or did would involve Mary Lester, a girl he loved in spite of everything.

2

MARY LESTER was fighting back tears of bitterness. Suddenly she wheeled from the ranch house window. She had watched Clay Mandell ride over the crest of the outward trail and her heart was a whirl of confused emotions.

"You — you awful fools!" she cried. "You're making everything worse!"

Rolf Lester looked back at her angrily. Seth Mundy stroked the leering smile on his dirty face with his equally dirty fingers.

"You needn't worry none, Mary," snapped Rolf. "The bullion is a-goin' out of here at sundown. No feller knows it's here."

"Sure right, Miss Lester," sneered Seth Mundy. "Like the boss told me to do. I made a wide trail out by the salt lake. Sure figure no galoot saw me driving that buck-board."

"Your boss," she said scornfully. "I wish I knew the name of this boss. I'd tell him he can't use the Circle Four as a dumping place for his robberies."

"Reckon you'll have to play the business our way, Mary," said Rolf harshly. "Some men were killed in that train robbery and — "

"Did you help to derail the train?" she flung at him.

"I've told you I was in Waco."

She rounded on Seth. "But you were there. You helped to kill men. There's too much violence in Waco: too much lawlessness all around this Texas territory."

"That what your deputy friend told you?" sneered Rolf Lester. "You'll have to drop that guy, sister. I don't like him."

She suddenly wanted to defend Clay Mandell but hardly knew what to say. "Oh, what can I do? I don't like this situation . . . "

Rolf took out the makings for a

cigarette and sent a grim glance to Seth Mundy. The bravado induced by his consumption of cheap whisky had now drained from him and he was just a grim man with a twisted mind.

"You can do nothing, Mary, except keep your mouth shut. Like I said, the gold will go out at sundown. You can just forget about it until then. If the boss told Seth to keep it here, that's the way it is."

"The boss!" she breathed. "I hate him! He's had you and Tad work for him, given you easy money. You've neglected this ranch to go shooting and heaven knows what else. And now Tad's dead! Oh, I don't know what to do or what to think!"

"Don't think. And don't talk to that durned deputy. I tell you he's poison to the like of us, Mary. He's a snake. I've heard him boasting in the saloons as how he'd get the Lester fellers by making up to their sister. That's the snake he is."

Mary went white-faced. "I can't

31

believe that of Clay . . . "

Rolf Lester went on angrily. "You got to believe it. He got Tad, didn't he? Killed him, just as he figures to do to me: only I pack a fast gun an' he'd better watch it."

"I wish you wouldn't talk like this."

"I'll get that Clay Mandell afore he gets me," boasted Rolf Lester.

It was more than the girl could stand. She rushed out of the big living room, where cut pine logs provided stout walls, and went into the kitchen. Blindly, she busied herself with her interrupted cooking. Her mind was a turmoil of thought, unable to think straight, and the only outstanding facts were the ones her brother had hammered at her.

Tad was dead. He was buried out there in the arid lands. Not even a Christian burial! It was too much. And Clay Mandell was the man who had hunted him down! That thought was as awful as her brother's death.

There had been a time a few

weeks back, when life had been fairly placid for a week or two, when she had thought she was falling in love with Clay. But Tad and Rolf had made her doubt him. And now all reasonable thought and emotion had been violently turned upside down. She was trying to hate Clay — but found she could not!

For an hour she found jobs to do in the kitchen, trying to chase out of her mind the knowledge that four boxes of stolen gold were hidden in the ranch-house cellar, beneath her very feet. The thought of it was sheer agony. Every few minutes she stopped working to stare out of a window, expecting the sound of hoofbeats to herald the arrival of a posse. But the hours sped by and the lawmen didn't come.

Rolf and Seth hung around the ranch-yard, smoking hand-rolled cigarettes incessantly. Angrily, she considered they could find work to do on the ranch because many jobs had been neglected lately. Way out along the valley, there were water-holes to clean out and some fence to mend. She thought some of their cattle had strayed far and wide. Rolf and Seth should be out checking on the steers. Oh, there was a lot of work to do — and it wasn't woman's work!

The hot burning sun, usual at this time in Texas, went down on the horizon. Rolf and Seth had the buckboard ready in the yard. The men walked around with Colts sagging heavily against their thighs. It seemed they were ready for trouble. Often the men peered out over the sage-covered land to the distant butte which marked the turn of the trail, but no rider came along. Then it was dark, with only a suspicion of light glowing across the sky from a hidden moon.

The gold was hauled out of the cellar and loaded on to the creaking buckboard. That work kept the men busy.

"Helluva lot of ounces of gold in each box," grunted Rolf.

"Reckon it could set a galoot up nicely," suggested Seth slyly. "Some weight there. I could barely lift each box."

Rolf's face was hidden under the shadows of his broad-brimmed hat. He answered the other sharply. "You'll get your pay. If you think you're smart enough to double-cross the boss, forget it. He would get you with lead — not gold. Reckon you ought to know that."

"I was only talkin'."

"Wal, quit talking and get moving. You got your orders from the boss, not me. You know you've got to meet two hombres with pack-horses out by Pike's Buttes. I'll go with you just in case you figure to risk your darned neck by shooshaying with that gold."

"You know I was only talking," snarled the man again. "I know blamed well I got to meet them hell-bent gents with pack-horses. Then fellers are taking the gold over the hills to

Pueblo where the boss has got buyers, I reckon."

"Don't reckon too much," snapped Rolf Lester. "It ain't so healthy, Seth. You just obey orders, huh. Let's get going." He threw his cigarette stub to the ground and then stamped on it, which was the habit in this land in summer.

The buckboard rattled out of the ranch-yard and went swiftly out on to the trail, with Rolf Lester riding ahead.

At a curtained window, Mary Lester watched it go with a feeling of relief and yet another feeling of dread. For where there was gold in this lawless land there was death, she knew. And more so with stolen gold.

Seth Mundy drove the buckboard, whipping the horses to full effort. Rolf Lester was a careful figure, sometimes ahead and other times alongside.

As they left the cottonwoods behind, and headed out along a rock-strewn trail that led to the arid lands that steadily encroached on the sparse grass of the Circle Four, a rider moved his horse carefully from out of the deep shadows of the big cottonwoods.

Clay Mandell turned in his saddle and his keen grey eyes searched the ranch buildings a few hundred yards away. Seeing no movement, he jigged his horse forward and went after the buckboard. Although the night had engulfed it, he could still hear the creaks and rattles of the springs.

He had spent the afternoon sleeping. He felt vastly better for the rest, almost a new man. While Sheriff Hoot Sampson had had a posse scouring the trails for sign of heavily-laden horses, he had kept his own counsel. He had told the sheriff nothing about seeing the boxes at the Circle Four that afternoon. He had gone against his duty and his conscience, but he had kept grimly to certain intentions.

He had seen it clearly. The gold consignment had been taken to the ranch as a temporary measure because the sheriff's men were out everywhere looking for the bandits. It had been obvious to him that the gold would stay concealed until nightfall. Clay had been so sure of his reasoning that he had calmly lain down and slept, leaving instructions for someone to waken him an hour or so before sundown.

There was one thing he wished to avoid. He did not want a posse tramping over the Circle Four ranch-house and throwing rough questions at Mary. He just did not want that and he stilled all questions and doubts in his mind.

He rode along the rocky trail, allowing the horse to pick its own way, knowing it was a sure-footed animal. The sounds from the distant buckboard drifted back to him in the otherwise silent night. Sound did travel far in darkness. He did not wish to get too close for that reason. He had to find out where the stolen gold was destined. More important than grabbing Seth Mundy or Rolf Lester was the chance that he might get closer to the men who employed them.

For Clay knew, as did Hoot Sampson and others in high office in Waco, that many of the robberies and shootings were planned by some big boss. When Tad Lester had slipped up, he had been working on his own, probably without approval from this big boss gent. There had been few slip ups when the boss-man planned an illegal event. The man who hired the gun-happy lawless men of Waco could be any one of three or four unscrupulous, big-time men in the town. There was Lansing, who owned the Bonanza Saloon, where anything went on from sudden death to all-night gambling. There was Tipping who was one of the gamblers, invariably winning, and with the back-up of gun-hands. And there were others, loners, men with fingers in many pies. But Hoot Sampson had not a legal thing on any one of them.

Clay rode on, his face shadowed under his pulled-down hat. He took a chance and left the trail, and rode across sage and mesquite covered ground to a distant pileup of rocks. He figured he could get closer to the moving buckboard this way and stay in the cover of the rocks.

The upthrust of rocky crags rose like an ugly sentinel into the dark sky. Clay jigged his horse slowly around the pileup. Then he reined in the animal, patting the tough hide affectionately so that it would not whinny.

He saw the buckboard drive past, with the horse pulling the load slowly. He figured that Seth Mundy had worked the animal too hard already.

But there was a lone rider with Seth. In the dark it had been hard to identify this rider but Clay was now sure it was Rolf Lester. So there were two to contend with!

Some minutes later Clay had crossed to the cover of an adjacent butte. Grass was thin here but enough to sustain any animal prepared to forage. There was an occasional bellow in the night from some distant cattle, maybe Circle Four animals; and a distant coyote howled at the obscured moon in the night.

The chase went on for some miles and then the terrain became jagged with towering buttes. This locality was known as Pike's Buttes, after some old crazy prospector who'd spent most of his life looking vainly for gold. Clay eased his mount well into the shadows of the rising mounds of rock and earth. He had the buckboard well in sight with the aid of a faint glow of light from the horizon when he suddenly heard subdued voices.

He realised men were greeting each other. The buckboard had stopped moving. He did not hear any of the groans and creaking sounds that had been emanating from it. He edged his horse further down the bluff until he could go no further without leaving the cover of the butte.

He could see the flare of sulphur matches as men lit smokes. As his eyes got the range in the gloom, he saw dark blotches which were horses. He identified a number of riderless animals and he suddenly realised they must be pack animals. He saw, fairly clearly now, two other riders in addition to Rolf Lester and Seth.

Clay eased a rifle from the saddle holster. He vaulted to the ground and hitched his reins to a jagged spur of rock. He did not fancy a spooked horse tearing into the night and leaving him.

He was pretty certain he could not approach any closer to the party of owl-hoots without giving away his advantage of surprise.

He would have to start shooting: maybe he could repossess the gold; maybe he could kill some of the bandits and send the others riding out in a scare: it was a risky kind of chance. But the play had run as far as he could allow it. He either took these men on or he rode off to fight another day. Maybe that was the prudent way.

Clay Mandell decided to hell with that kind of caution.

He crouched behind a convenient boulder, away from his horse because he did not want a dead animal if the men started firing back, which they surely would.

He sighted his Winchester carefully on one of the new riders. He had no idea who the man might be in the dark and he thought grimly that he did not care. He triggered the rifle.

Crack! The steel-jacketed shell flashed out in a spit of yellow flame and Clay triggered again and saw a distant rider in the gloomy night pitch from his horse. That man had fallen victim to the first bullet and had been slow in falling, strangely coinciding with the second shot.

"Dead, I figure," muttered Clay, "but that second shot kinda missed. Damn!"

As the men out yonder scattered with sudden yells and oaths, he chanced off another shot from his Winchester. A good accurate rifle in the hands of a marksman gave Clay results. The shot echoed strongly in the silent night air, the buttes sending the sound back across the land. And he'd got another rider. He saw the dark shape topple slowly from the saddle with a dragging motion. So two men were down, just targets, gun fodder, he thought grimly. Who had he got? Maybe they were Seth or Rolf! Maybe!

By that time, just seconds after his shots, the two other men had flattened down on to the hard earth. The pack horses had spooked and, snorting wildly, were running in all directions.

Colt flame spat from the distance but Clay merely smiled at this retaliation. He was out of the range of a six-shooter. He levelled his rifle over the rock and searched keenly through the night air for a target. All he wanted was the slightest movement from one of the flattened men out there. He was out to get these gents. They were hell-bents and beyond the law.

He saw a Colt spit flame and he

triggered at it immediately. As the echoes died away, he listened for a cry of pain but none came to his ear. Obviously he had missed.

The horse hitched to the buckboard was rearing wildly, trying to get movement, and then it got under way. In the faint blue light he saw the animal gallop away towards a grassy defile, but then the gloom became too deep and the buckboard was invisible to him.

The Colts out ahead were silent now. Worse than that, he could not be sure if he could actually see the two men. There were deceptive patches, which sometimes made him raise his rifle and aim, but they turned out to be rocks. Maybe the two rogues were lying with the immobility of rocks. Grimly, he waited and peered ahead, hoping for something to show signs of movement.

But as the silence continued he realised that the other two men had crept away across the hard grass and semi-arid land, probably moving like snakes on their bellies.

Clay went on, moving slowly and determinedly across the land to the spot where he judged the two dead men lay. As he came closer, he knew that the horses had all gone off in fright. He went on, rifle ready and finger on the trigger. The slightest movement ahead and the rifle would challenge it instantly with sudden death!

But he came upon the two bodies without a shot or movement to startle him. He examined the first one, a typical range ruffian, white and dirty. Clay did not know him. Maybe he was from Waco and maybe not. The man had the stamp of hired gun-hand written all over him. He was also very dead. Perhaps a bit of lucky shooting!

Clay discovered the second galoot. He was a Mexican, away from his border homeland it seemed. The man was bad hit and dying and religious oaths issued from his lips. Clay tried to reposition the man, make him comfortable, but he was too far gone.

The sudden drum of hoofs caused Clay to drop to one knee and level his rifle. He thought he could see the dark shape of galloping animals far away against the deep black gloom of a rising hillock and he fired swiftly, grimly. He emptied the rifle and then stopped to reload. The hoof-beats continued to drum out and a horse whinnied in fright.

Obviously this time he had hit nothing.

He ran back for his own horse. He knew that the two men had crept away until they had caught up with the spooked horses. Now they were making their escape.

By the time Clay got to his cayuse and leaped into the saddle, the night had swallowed up the other riders. He cursed, forgetting that he had done well to stop the owlhoots' play. He rode on, slowly, carefully in the night, although for some reason there was a little bit more illumination from a fugitive moon. All at once there came to his ears the snorting of a horse in fright and the lashing of hoofs on hard rock and the loud rattling of a straining buckboard.

He rowelled his mount and, seconds later, saw the shape of the buckboard ahead. The horse was rearing and kicking. The big wheels of the carriage had jammed in a tight groove among some rocks.

There was nothing else to do but give up the chase for the other men and calm the horse. Then he manoeuvred the wheel out of the groove and backed the buckboard on to some flat grass land.

He examined the load. There were four long boxes, just as he had seen carried into the ranch-house earlier that day, and they answered to the description Hoot Sampson had given him.

Branded on one side with a burning iron was the legend *Dorado Gold Company*.

The weight of each box was considerable, enough for one man to handle for normal lifting purposes. There was a lot of gold in each box, worth a lot of money: and in fact gold was money. The boxes were the type that were lined with tin-plate to prevent loss of precious gold dust, but he guessed there were canvas bags inside the boxes. This was some consignment!

He hitched his own horse to the rear of the carriage and then climbed onto the box. He took up the traces and commenced to drive off with the now calmer animal between the shafts. He passed some hillocks of rock, sand and grass, driving with his rifle in one hand and the leathers in the other.

"Now what the heck do I tell Hoot Sampson?" he muttered, this thought uppermost in his troubled mind.

It seemed he'd have to tell the truth because a load of Dorado gold had to be accounted for, and somehow he'd try to minimise the role the girl had played in all this. Of course she could not remain unaffected if Rolf Lester was hauled into custody and made to account for his actions. Did the buckboard belong to the Lesters? Maybe. It seemed that Rolf and Seth had the luck of their kind for they had not stopped a bullet in the recent gun-play, so far as he knew.

Clay drove down from the buttes and hilly land and found the trail that led through the clumps of mesquite and sage. A little amount of watery moon made his passage a bit easier. That was his luck because driving a buckboard in the dark was full of hazards, especially with some weight, and he'd be up the creek if the animal went lame.

He entered Waco township, driving the carriage slowly down the main stem, not wishing to attract attention. Yellow oil-light spilled from some saloons where the customers were habitually fond of late entertainment and all-night card games when the money was available. A honky-tonk piano came to his ear and he smiled wryly, thinking it was a long time since he'd enjoyed some rough pleasures. Lately life had seemed to be all work and duty.

Some cowboys were in Waco, whooping it up, probably because it was pay-day for them. Some gold miners from the Rio Pecos river only twenty miles away were probably in town, he could guess, exchanging their gold dust straight over the counter for rotgut rye. And there'd be a few of the Irish railroad workers, ready to drink and fight. There were, of course, just as many hard-working traders and ranchers seeking some pleasure and escape from their laborious lives. Most of the people knew the value of living and working in the protection of a town where there was some law, but of course a town like Waco attracted the other type.

Clay found Hoot Sampson at the office, a cigarette in his mouth, his hat on the desk and his boots off.

"Taking it easy?" grinned Clay.

"You said it! Been riding and stamping around all blasted day after them mangy railroad bandits. No trail no-how! Guess we was too late getting there, but how the hell do we know there's going to be a holdup? Railroad guards didn't see the bullion get away either. Pesky mystery . . . "

Clay considered his thoughts; what kind of words could he use? He'd just have to come right out with it, he decided. "You can stop worrying about that damned gold, Hoot."

"You don't say!"

"I've got the gold outside!"

"Are you kiddin' me?" raged the sheriff.

"No joke, Hoot. Get your boots on. You can give me a hand. I don't feel easy with those boxes lying on a buckboard, although I've covered them with some straw.

His announcement got Hoot Sampson's boots on in record time. In some fast movements they were outside the office examining the bullion boxes.

"Reckon that's them!"

"Feel the weight. They're full — and I don't figure it's useless rock."

Hoot Sampson stared at his deputy. "How come? How come you just ride in here with a consignment of gold-stolen gold?"

"Help me in with them, Hoot. Then I'll give you the play."

They got the boxes inside the office. Once again Clay thought that each single box was as much as a man could handle, so it seemed there was a small fortune in gold. Hoot locked the boxes in one of the cells and then stared questioningly at his deputy.

Clay began speaking slowly, searching for careful words. He told the sheriff that he had ridden out to the trail that went past the Circle Four ranch, that he had seen the buckboard being driven out into the hilly semi-arid lands, and how he had killed two men waiting for it.

"Who was driving the buckboard out?" the sheriff wanted to know.

"Reckon it was Rolf Lester and his sidekick, Seth Mundy," said Clay quietly.

"Lester, huh! That hellion! Just like his brother Tad — and the old man, for that! How come you was so lucky to jump them?"

"Guess I wanted to see Mary Lester."

There were gaps in the story and Hoot Sampson looked puzzled.

"What made you ride out that way, son?"

"I've told you, I wanted to see Mary."

"Huh! Heard you went over there at midday — but no matter. You've done fine, Clay. Could be a reward for this gold."

"I don't want it. Just doing my job."

The sheriff frowned. "Hey, now, don't get too high-handed about money, my boy! Wal, reckon we'll see if we can pick up those two rogues Rolf and Seth. Might be lucky. They keep late hours in the saloons. More often than not when they should be working I hear. But I want the man behind these lawless doings. If I got the man those two are working for I'd nail his hide to a barn door with pleasure. That's the feller I want."

Clay had to wait until the sheriff got a man to stand guard on the office. Then the two went out into Waco's streets. Before they walked off, they looked at the buckboard thoughtfully and then got the liveryman at the back of the office to take it in charge.

"Maybe we can get someone to identify that buckboard as belonging to the Lesters? Could be some sort of evidence . . . "

Clay nodded, thinking that this involved Mary. It was going to be difficult to shield her.

"If it's Lester's, should be simple to pin that on him," Clay muttered slowly.

They had their horses, just in case they were needed, and they walked them slowly down the main street of Waco. "Figure we'll look in at the Bonanza Saloon. Won't take more'n a minute. If we're wasting our time — okay."

"That's Rolf Lester's place these days," said Clay.

"Yeah. Drinks too much for a young galoot. I heard you had a fight with him. Want me to jug him for that?"

"Nope."

"Suit yourself. Me, I'd be happy if that young cuss was plumb dead — and sure as hell he will be some day soon. Like his damned brother!"

Clay was silent.

"Reckon we'll have to visit the Circle Four maybe tomorrow, continued the sheriff. "Ask about that buckboard, huh?"

Again silent, Clay simply nodded.

The Bonanza Saloon was fairly well patronised for the time of night when they pushed a way inside. Noise and yellow oil-light greeted them, a contrast to the night air.

"Sure like a drink myself," grunted Hoot Sampson. "But some of these men just go crazy for more whisky until they are topped to their damned sombreros! Well, what d'you know! Look what we got!"

Clay, too, had seen the men. He didn't need the sheriff's idle words to see that Rolf Lester and Seth Mundy were present, something he found hard to believe after all the riding they had put in. The two men were leaning unconcernedly on the mahogany. Clay walked in slowly, grimly, and the two men looked hard at him. Clay noticed the tightness of their mouths although they attempted to manage a sneering sort of smile. It was, of course, derision.

Sheriff Hoot Sampson shouldered up. "You hell-bent gents were out in the wilds a few hours ago. Do you aim to come along quietly to the cells, or what?"

"What the hell are you yapping about, Sheriff?"

"I'm talking about gold — missing gold."

And Hoot Sampson's Colt came out of the holster as if by magic. The red-moustached sheriff could draw with the swiftest in Waco. He had been a sheriff for a long time for that simple and sound reason.

"You figure to come quietly?" he asked.

To back him up, Clay eased his gun into the palm of his hand.

Rolf Lester allowed a smile to flit over his hard face. He uttered the short sneering laugh which was characteristic. He winked at Seth Mundy and even settled back comfortably against the bar counter.

The hubbub in the saloon subsided a bit as men watched and momentarily stopped talking. But others were unconcerned because gun-handling was not uncommon. Some hardly looked up. Others continued drinking. But some wary individuals eased away from the scene.

"You sure got your loop tangled, Sheriff," sneered Rolf. "We ain't been anywhere this night. Not so that we know about it!" And he laughed mockingly.

Seth Mundy's evil-lined visage creased in a grin.

"Reckon you can put that gun away, Mister Sampson," he said in mock civility. "Heck, a feller can't drink in peace. Don't know what this burg is coming to."

Hoot Sampson's mouth set grimly. He looked down at Rolf Lester's boots and then at Seth's scrubbed footwear.

"You got riding dust on your boots."

The two hard-cases made a pretence of staring at their high-heeled riding boots. Sure enough there was a great deal of yellowish dust, the kind that got stirred up out in the semi-arid lands.

"Wal, now, if that ain't dust! Any feller here got dust on his boots? Sheriff don't like it! Heh! Heh!"

There was some laughter at Rolf's

joke. Other men in the saloon looked uneasy.

Clay shot a hard glance at the sheriff. "Maybe these galoots don't know what it's all about," he suggested. "Maybe they figure we're kidding."

Hoot Sampson lost his temper. "You know blamed well you've been shooting it out with Clay here! We've got your buckboard, and the gold that was stolen from the wrecked railroad car. I'm asking you two to come along to the office to answer questions. Are you two pests a-coming?"

"Nope," snapped Rolf Lester. "We ain't been out in the hard lands and this dust has been on my boots for days. Same as Seth. He likes dust. You can see that any time! He's one dusty hombre!"

"Quit fooling!" snapped Clay.

"But we ain't," jeered Rolf. "Reckon you'd better ask Dave Lansing where we been this day, Sheriff. Do it before that gun pops and Clay has to put you in the hoosegow."

The mocking answers were almost too much and Hoot Sampson was becoming very angry. But there was movement in the saloon and the man called Dave Lansing came close to Clay and the sheriff.

"These boys have been playing cards all night," said the man easily. "With me — and a friend."

Dave Lansing was a burly saturnine fellow in a black gambler's suit. He wore a clean white shirt of some distinction and a black necktie, his hands were soft and white and as supple as a woman's, he sported a curt moustache which gave him an air of spurious dignity. He smiled placatingly at Clay and the sheriff.

"Rolf and Seth were in my little back room," he elaborated. "They are two gents I can vouch for. They've been with me most of the day and night — won some money, too." He paused. "We've got other witnesses who can swear to that."

3

SHERIFF Hoot Sampson put his gun back in his shiny holster with a very slow deliberation, as if to signify the end of the matter.

"You really mean that, Lansing? You're prepared to swear that on oath?"

Lansing had surprise on his suave face. "Sure do. I tell you the boys have been playing cards with me and Secker and MacBride over there. You want to talk to them?"

"Alibis, huh? You've got it all figured out: but I know when a man is lying; and lies tell me something about a gent. Let's go, Clay . . . "

They turned without another word and walked through the few patrons in the saloon. On few faces was there much sympathy for the lawmen, because most of the hard men present thought the whole thing rather amusing. Few of them knew much in the way of detail, but the sheriff and his deputy had been made to look like fools and that was good enough for the type present.

The lawmen returned to the office and at a nod the other guard left for the night. "Wal, at least we got the gold." Clay took off his gunbelt.

"Them fellers had it all figured out," grunted the sheriff, indignantly. "And me having to put my gun back in the leather! That Dave Lansing is sure a fine liar. But I've known that for some time."

"You can say that again," agreed Clay. "Because it was Rolf and Seth I saw driving out with the buckboard. Maybe we can trip Lansing with that. Maybe we can prove that the carriage belongs to the Circle Four. Must be some guy who can testify to that . . . "

Hoot Sampson was frowning, searching his pockets for the makings. "I don't get everything straight, Clay. Where was the gold all the blamed afternoon? How come those two men were taking it out into the wastelands at night? I had men out on all the damned known trails — men I'd sworn in as temporary possemen — and they were looking for riders and any sign of that gold."

"Reckon they must have had it hidden." Clay cut short on any other explanations. He was still grimly intent upon keeping Mary Lester out of this. If it were known she had helped the men hide the gold, she might have to answer serious charges. Okay, he was fudging his duty, but this was a hard land and a man made his own decisions.

"Wal, the gold goes back to the Dorado Gold Company tomorrow," declared Hoot. "Hope they get the blasted stuff away this time. Gold and grief — they go together."

Although it was late they had a visitor to the office. He was Malcolm Starn, a freight-line owner in Waco. "I was in that bar, Sheriff, and I saw your play with them hombres. Me, I don't like that Lester feller, or his sidekick, Seth Mundy. A third-rate rogue, that one. What was wrong, Hoot? Anything I can do to help?"

The sheriff looked at the medium-sized man in the clean store suit; saw his inquiring grey eyes and honest face. He liked Malcolm Starn well enough, knowing him as a good businessman who was not too talkative about his affairs. But the man had a sound reputation. He did not drink a lot and did not wear a gun. Except for the fact that he was in business, Hoot Sampson did not really know much more about him. The man was frequently out of town and perhaps that accounted for his lack of background.

"It ain't much," muttered the sheriff. "We got the gold consignment back that was stolen from the derailed train, and we figured that Lester and his grubby pal had plenty to do with it."

"Got the gold? That's fine." Malcolm Starn took out a little snuff-box and held it out invitingly to the two others.

They declined with a smile but Starn took a generous dose.

"Glad to hear you're keeping these gun-happy fools in order, Sheriff," he observed. "They'll meet a bad end sooner or later, of course, and we'll be rid of 'em. I reckon I've lost out on some of these holdups myself, in one way or another — "

Hoot Sampson stared. "You never reported anythin'."

"Yeah, wal, I'm going. I've had enough drink for one night."

Clay Mandell got to his feet. "Just a moment, Mister Starn. You're in the freight business, know all about carts and carriages; would you come around to the livery behind the office for a minute? Maybe you could look at this buckboard and maybe identify it."

Starn nodded. "Anything to oblige the law. I reckon men in this town can't do decent business without law and order. So I support you men all the way. Yessir! And it's right enough: I supply a lot of buckboards around

66

Waco. I can tell you who built them just by looking."

"I figured you could, Starn," said Clay, looking speculatively at the man.

The three men went around to the back of the building. With the aid of a lantern, Starn spent some time examining the buckboard which Clay had brought in.

"One thing's sure," stated Malcolm Starn. "I didn't sell this buggy."

"Can you identify it as belonging to Rolf Lester at the Circle Four?" asked Clay grimly.

Starn hesitated. "I can't say it belongs to him. Maybe it does and maybe it don't. But I didn't supply it. Never went through my hands, not this one."

Clay nodded. "All right, Mister Starn. We'll just keep at it. We might pin the ownership of this buggy on Rolf Lester. By that I mean papers of ownership — you know, a bill of sale."

"And then the cuss will reckon it

was stolen from their ranch," growled the sheriff. "Aw, heck — this ain't the same as catching them red-handed."

The two lawmen returned to the office and Starn went back to his bachelor home behind his freight office.

"Bit of a mystery man," observed Clay. "I don't know a lot about Mister Starn . . ."

"Reckon we could say that about plenty of gentry in this town," muttered Hoot Sampson. "What with comings an' goings, we don't know the half of it."

Clay nodded. Then the sheriff said: "Look hyar, my lad, you'd better get some more shut-eye. That spell you had this afternoon ain't no use to a big galoot like yourself."

Clay had to agree. He returned up the stairs to the upper storey where he had his room. He took off his boots and hung up his gunbelt like a western man, and then rolled on to the bunk and immediately fell asleep.

It seemed hardly minutes later, but

it might have been a good hour, when he was awakened by the blasting of Colt guns.

He jumped up, thrust into alertness, found his boots and thrust his belt around his waist in swift motion. He moved swiftly down the stairs to join the enraged sheriff.

"Goldarn this town! A man can't get any rest. Now what the hell is this!"

The sudden crash of glass and the whine of a Colt slug made them duck.

"Broken the cussed window!" roared Hoot.

Clay had his six-shooter palmed. Carefully, crouching low, he moved around the office and got behind the desk as another window crashed as a slug broke through. Clay listened for another minute. "Reckon there's three or maybe four gun-happy gents out there," he stated.

"What's the damned idea?" roared Hoot Sampson. "Ain't these hell-bents got no use for the law? What's the idea of shootin' up the sheriff's office? An' look at the damage! Gawd-blast!" He was more enraged about broken glass than any possibility of personal injury.

Clay moved to the gaping hole in the window. He poked a Colt over the ledge and waited for a target. Suddenly a gun roared and flame lanced momentarily, but it was enough for the deputy. He triggered instantly at the gun shot.

He was rewarded by a sudden scream of pain and vile curses. Clay grinned with satisfaction and moved away from the window in case some gun-toter outside was about to sight his gun-flame. He left the sheriff at the other window, snapping shots out into the darkness, making plenty of din but not finding anything substantial.

Then Clay went down the passage that led to the cells. At the end of this passage was a door which was seldom opened, being bolted and barred. He withdrew the rusty bolt and took down the cross-bar, slipping out into the back yard of the building. On the right was the small livery.

He got behind a water-butt and crouched. Across the way he could see the dim figure of a man standing close to the post that supported the false front of the nearby building.

Clay took careful aim and fired.

He saw the man spin ludicrously round the post and sink to the ground as if in agony.

Clay stepped swiftly across the way and crouched beside the man. The first thing that he noticed was the strong stink of drink on the guy, as if he was really topped up. Clay thought vaguely that he knew this rannigan. Yeah, he was a bar loafer who worked when money became tight for him, known in the saloons and not too fussy about what work he did to get his dinero. He did not know the man's name.

Clay sidled along the boardwalk of the nearby building and stared across the road. There was a certain amount of light spilling from a saloon, enough to see a man hugging the wall of a building next to it. Clay waited until the man poked a long-barrelled Colt around the corner of the wall. Then Clay moved his own gun and sent death crashing across the road. He saw the man stagger backwards under the impact of the heavy slug, falling to the ground and squirming horribly, crying out in pain. Then the man lay still. Clay felt grimly that gun-death was a dirty business.

There was a sudden movement in general as if the last man to die had been a signal. Horses' hoofs drummed all at once. Nearby a horse snorted in fear and pawed in fright at dirt. Suddenly two men rode big mounts out of the alleys opposite the sheriff's office and desperately rowelled the creatures into a full lope.

Hoot Sampson appeared at the office main door, emptying his gun at the departing men. It was a gesture of rage with little chance of hitting anything.

"Damned gun-toting villains!"

If his horse had been saddled and available, he would have gone after the men. But the animal was in the livery and there was no time to do anything effective.

Clay knew the ruckus was over. He went along to the ruffians he had shot. Again he was looking at a typical gun-wearing hard-case and another gentleman of the same type. They were the type of men who could be hired when filled with whisky. They were not known to him but maybe they were not galoots who had been in Waco very long.

Clay came away in sudden distaste. Blood and the smell of death were pretty sickening things at close range.

He rejoined Hoot Sampson at the office door and stood grimly. One or two range men had emerged from the saloons, now that the shooting had died away, and were staring curiously.

"This place will be known as boothill town if this goes on," muttered Clay. "I'll go along and tell the town grave-digger that we've got two dead customers for him."

"Is this town civilised or ain't it?" fumed Hoot Sampson. "We got a railroad and a telegraph, an' pretty soon we'll have a newspaper. Yessir, a real print works: an' there was a man in Waco the other week taking photographs — that's what he called em. Real pictures! Huh!"

Clay grinned. "They've been doing that back east for a long time, Hoot."

"We've got the chance to make Waco a fine town. There's good range out there, even if the grass is a bit thin right now with the ground being hard. There's gold in the hills — although I'm durned if I know if that's a blessing. I reckon cattle is the best thing for Waco. But what do we get? A lot of damned gunslingers who think shooting off their smokepoles is more important that progress." Hoot paused. "Now why did they create all that ruckus?"

"Hired gun hands." Clay stated. "But who hired them — and why? I'd like to know the identity of the fellers who got away. As I say, Hoot, I think they were after the gold."

"If we'd been killed, the Texas Rangers would have moved in to keep law and order," said the sheriff. "That would scare the gunslicks, I guess. Gold, you say? How the heck did those dirty rannies expect to take the gold?"

"Well, if we'd been shot to hell, four riders could take a box up on each horse, no problem," said Clay dryly. "Maybe that was the idea — but two of 'em are dead."

"Or maybe some gent just gave orders to shoot us out of existence," snarled Hoot. "I figure there's some man behind these gun-happy fools."

Two men strolled over at this point to give a critical inspection of the bullet holes in the office building. One was Dave Lansing from the Bonanza Saloon, the other was Doc Hawton, a quiet studious man with an unsmiling expression. Both men were the type who wore store suits, with expensive waistcoats, and they certainly were not range men.

"Seems you are getting mighty unpopular, Sheriff," drawled Lansing. "Why all the shooting?"

"I wouldn't know," snarled Hoot, trying to cover up. He stroked his bristly red moustache and said thoughtfully: "Go get back an' get yourself an alibi, Lansing."

"I don't need to perform such tricks, Sheriff." His dark eyes swept over the office structure. "Guess the taxes will rise next year in this town to pay for this damage."

As he strolled away, Doc Hawton shook his head in despair. He hooked his fingers in his vest and spoke sepulchrally. "I hear there are more dead men. There is too much violence. Why can't you keep law and order, Sheriff? Every day I am dressing wounds. It's too bad."

"Good for your business, Doc," snapped Hoot and Clay grinned. The sheriff went back to his room, now

76

that there was peace and quiet in the night.

After Clay had got the grave-digger to heave the dead men away, he returned to his bunk, tired, utterly exhausted in a sudden way as he patted his bed.

This time he went to sleep with his gunbelt around him and the weapon in the leather. It was not very comfortable but maybe it was safer!

4

THE next day the gold was deposited with officials of the Dorado Gold Company, whose main gold source in the county was the mine near the Rio Pecos River, some forty miles away from Waco. Two years ago the company had bought out all the mineral rights for a long way around, and sent the panning miners packing and installed machinery to crush ore, something the prospectors could not do, and the gold was coming out well. Some of Waco's leading traders and others had bought shares in the company.

Clay Mandell found time to ride out to the Circle Four the next day. As he came over the sage and mesquite studded lands, he was aware of a rising wind, with the cloudless sky taking on an increasingly brassy colour. The wind was pressing ominously on from one direction. There was all the sign of a blow, or to be more precise a turbulence. In this area of Texas they were a regular thing at certain times of the year.

A long time later, when the ranch-house came into view, at the end of the grassy valley where cattle moved slowly, he urged his mount into a canter and came quickly into the ranch-yard.

He could not see Rolf or Seth. For that he was thankful. If he could, he'd like to avoid confrontation.

A few minutes later he was talking to Mary Lester on the front porch. She closed the door behind her, her face set but a troubled look in her lovely eyes.

"What do you want, Clay?"

"Listen, Mary," he rushed into words. "I know all about the gold being here — "

"You knew?"

She looked suddenly helpless, the set expression vanishing.

"I saw the boxes being taken in by Seth," he said. "And I followed them that night, out into the wastelands. We swopped lead and two men got killed — a bad thing — no pleasure to me. But Rolf could have got his uppance that night: and what would you have thought of me?"

She looked helpless.

"Killer — or friend?" he pursued angrily.

"Why do you tell me all this?" she whispered.

"I just want you to understand, Mary, that I'll help you if and when you need it. I'm not here to hound you . . . "

"You're here to pick up Rolf," she accused.

He smiled wryly. "Nope. Your brother got himself a nice alibi last night. A gent by the name of Dave Lansing swore Rolf and that scrubby gent, Seth, were in a back room at the Bonanza Saloon playin' cards all night. As that is a pack of lies, it figures Dave

Lansing is playing a funny game. But Rolf and Seth have witnesses — even if they are liars — to prove they weren't out in the wastelands. That's the kind of gents your brother is mixed up with, Mary, no-good rogues."

"Does the sheriff know about the gold being here?"

"I kept that to myself. And me swearing on oath to uphold the law! So don't give yourself away with careless words, Mary."

She stared past him, across the grass lands, sensing the rising wind.

"You'd better go before Rolf and Seth come back," she whispered.

"I just want to say this, Mary. Some day your brother is going to encounter big grief. To put it bluntly, if he keeps on gunslinging he'll get his come-uppance. He'll go for his gun once too often. I want to be able to help you when that happens, Mary, and don't let Rolf make you do anything against the law. I know of course you have too much intelligence to let that happen."

She was staring anxiously at the trail where it rounded the solitary butte on the Circle Four range. The wind was rising in intensity, and in the distance cattle were huddled together as tall grasses bent over.

Then: "You'd better go. Oh, here's Rolf! Please avoid trouble, Clay . . ."

He turned, nodding agreement but grimly feeling that trouble was inevitable. He walked down the porch steps to the dusty ranch-yard and waited until the other man rode up.

Rolf Lester swung down from his saddle and stamped over, arrogance in every stride he took. He grinned with savage confidence. "I don't like you around here, Mister Damned Lawman."

"I don't really want to be here. I only came to see Mary."

"An' you can git to hell outa here!" snarled the other.

"Sure. I'll get my hoss . . ."

"Maybe you'd like to take off your belt like you did the other, day — or maybe you're yellow like all badge-toters."

Clay's temper was rising in spite of his promise to the girl. The other man's confidence was so assured. He knew he had beaten Clay once before in a fist-battle. He gloated over the prospect of repeating this triumph. And this time there'd be no interfering rancher to prevent Clay's hand from being smashed up. The chance of unleashing some really dirty tricks in a fight filled Rolf Lester with savage satisfaction.

Rolf unhooked his gun-belt and hung it over a nearby fence. Sneering, his face was a give-away as to his intentions.

"You can't fight here!" cried Mary Lester.

"I'll teach this swine another lesson," snapped Rolf.

He figured to get quick advantage. As Clay was unbuckling his own gun-belt, the trouble-maker rushed in, swinging a left hook.

Clay jerked his head at the last second, dropping his gun-belt, but the blow rammed home and senses swam momentarily.

Clay had to back as he tried to shake the pain out of his head. Angry at being taken, he advanced towards this arrogant young buckeroo. The last time Rolf Lester had had it all his own way because of the tiredness that had permeated his very bones. But now he felt fierce and red-blooded.

He knew Mary was watching. Like any man worth his salt, he wasn't going to back down in front of a girl he admired.

Clay's arms rammed out with his angry confidence pushing him on into this challenge. He wanted to hurt Rolf Lester because he disliked the young upstart. Someone had to teach him a lesson.

Clay's fist rammed on the other's chin, jerking the man's head back. Then the other man barged in, ignoring the numerous blows. For a moment it seemed he had the edge. His arms hacked through the air, through Clay's guard, and hammered home at the body. Clay swung more blows, like a steam-hammer that never tires. He saw a split appear on the other guy's cheek and blood spurted. Then a rock-like fist staggered Clay and he went back against a fence.

Rolf Lester grinned like an Indian savage and drew his fist back for what he thought would be a pulverising blow. But Clay bounced from the springy fence and planted his fists into the other's eyes as if to smash flesh and bone. Blood spurted again and Rolf Lester's face became a reddened mask and Clay's fists were filthy with blood. Rolf made disgusting hissing sounds and he faltered, stood swaying. Then his fist swung out mechanically but missed a solid target because Clay jerked away in time.

Then Clay bored in with renewed determination. He hit out as if he was trying to knock down a tree. Rolf Lester staggered back, yard by yard, the blows thudding into him. They went across the ranch-yard in this fashion, slugging away, but the arrogant man getting by far the worst of the fight.

Mary watched helplessly.

Clay was not the man to forget that the Lester rannigan had beaten him in a fight once. He hated the recollection. It was the grim need to establish his own confidence that drove him to ram blow after blow into the face before him.

The sound of harsh grunts and animal noises plus the sound of slithering boots drifted over the ranch-yard. Rolf Lester, knowing he was being slowly beaten and punished, tried a few roughhouse tricks. He kicked out with a boot more than once. Clay jerked grimly, avoiding the kicks that could cripple him. Then he bored in again and landed two punishing punches that drew harsh panting sounds from the other man.

Rolf Lester backed up against a fence and threw out arms that were now moving slowly because of the haze in front of his eyes. His arms were like lead but he kept them up like bulwarks, trying to ward off Clay's grim punishing blows.

Then he began to slither down as his legs weakened, the fence his only support. Clay banged unmercifully at the man, fists ramming body and face. Rolf Lester's eyes closed and then jerked open in an effort to retain his senses. His mouth was open and twisted as he sucked desperately for breath. One arm was hooked around the fence, although he did not realise that.

Clay punched grimly again. With every slamming blow he felt grim satisfaction, knowing this man deserved a grim lesson. Rolf Lester stopped at nothing when things were going his way — even killing. So Clay did not intend to relent until this tough young man had tasted real punishment.

Clay did not see Seth Mundy ride into the yard. The man got off his horse and approached with a gait which was almost creeping.

Seth pulled a gun and stuck it in Clay's back.

"You can quit right now — or take a slug!"

Clay's arms fell and he stepped back with slow movements, like a man who is tired after terrific effort. Rolf Lester hung on to the fence and fought the mists that sickened his brain. Then, laboriously, he dragged himself up, swayed and wiped the blood from his mouth, glaring murder at Clay Mandell.

Clay eyed the dirty-looking Seth Mundy. "You can put that gun away. You're threatening a lawman. Another wrong move from you, hombre, an' I'll haul you all the way back to the hoosegow at Waco."

"Deputies have been shot to hell afore!" Seth itched to pull the trigger, but inwardly he was a coward who could only fight when everything was stacked in his favour.

They did not realise that Mary had

been to the house and got a rifle. The old gun with the shiny barrel looked menacing enough. Clay smiled wryly at the sight of it. He knew she wouldn't use it.

"Put that gun away, Seth Mundy. And you can get off this ranch, Clay Mandell. I won't have you fighting with my brother."

He smiled thinly. "Sorry you had to see this ruckus. But I owed that scrap to Rolf. Seems we kinda dislike each other."

"For goodness' sake get on your cayuse!" she cried. "And ride out of here. There's too much trouble . . . "

For a moment he saw tears spring to her eyes and he had the impulse to take her in his arms and comfort her. Sure thing, he had no desire to be antagonistic towards Mary Lester — although her hellion brother was a different matter. If only he could protect her! He was a western man who had a protective instinct towards womenfolk.

Seth Mundy had slid his weapon into leather and turned away, muttering and grinning in some sort of triumph. Clay walked to the fence, retrieved his gun-belt and strapped it on. Then he went over to his horse, grimly silent again. He leaped to the saddle and rode away without so much as a backward glance.

He had spoken his mind, told Mary about knowing the gold had been stashed away in the ranch-house. He had made it plain he wanted to help her and he had asked her not to do anything towards helping her brother which might make her ashamed later. More than this he could not do. He had obviously shown that he wanted to be her friend; more than that, when relations between them were better.

And there had been some satisfaction in beating Rolf Lester. God knows if that made him a better man — but he had done it! That the young hell-bent would hate him more than ever he did not doubt.

He began to notice the velocity of

the wind again. There was a howling sound in the distance as the wind surged around some rocky buttes and the air was full of grit. Seemed there was all the making of a storm with sand blowing in from the distant wastelands. This choking fine grit could be blown for miles, eventually settling when the storm was over on the grass lands.

The content of dust and grit increased and he slid his bandana up over his mouth and nose. The storm was on him. The visibility was becoming very poor and he could barely see the essential markers of the trail. With the horse plodding on gamely, he realised he could be momentarily lost in this type of dust storm. Grit stung his face. The animal whinnied in fright. For some time there was nothing but the driving screen of dust.

He realised the sand and dust were blowing in from the arid lands further east, travelling incredible distances and would settle on the grass. This sort of storm over the years could even affect the sparse grasslands of a ranch like the Circle Four and choke them. If this process went on for years, there would be a time when the ranch would be arid land itself. This had happened in other distant places miles from Waco. The desert could encroach.

He hunched in the saddle and let the horse plod on. He reckoned he was a good two hours out of Waco, maybe more if he had veered a lot from the direct trail. He could hardly recognise his surroundings; in fact he was at times lost, merely obeying a hunch as to his bearing. Somewhere ahead lay Waco but it was almost unbelievable how space could be condensed into a mere few yards of visibility ahead of him.

He hoped the storm would blow out. Maybe he should rest the animal. Maybe he should squat down in the shelter of some rocky outcrop, reassuring the cayuse. That was the usual trick practised by riders in a blow of this kind.

But the wind intensity continued, with dust and grit making the whole expedition a trial for man and brute. There was no real shelter. He might be within twenty yards of a rocky pile but he couldn't see. In face, he might be moving in a circle. The return to town was going to be a struggle.

Rider and horse braced against the harsh wind and plodded on against the abrasive screen of sand. Clay was about to dismount and pull the horse down to the ground for a rest, when, above the howl of the wind, he heard the sound of Colt gun-fire.

He reined his horse to a standstill, wondering if he had heard right. With sand in his eyes and ears, he might be suffering a delusion. A second later, with characteristic determination, he decided that he had heard a gun.

The crack came again through the yellowish air and he saw the stab of yellow flame from a gun. So he was close to the shooting!

And then, as he urged his animal

into movement again, he came upon an extraordinary scene enacted in the swirling storm.

Clay saw a man rise from the ground only yards from him and grab at a waiting horse. Another second and the man and rider disappeared in the driving sand-filled air. The man had urged the horse fiercely.

After another yard or two, Clay found the body of a man lying across his path, and the horse jigged instinctively to one side. Calming the brute, Clay dismounted and inspected the body. The man wore rough clothes, working gear, a tattered vest and dirt-stained trousers. Clay got the hunch he was not a cow-hand. There wasn't a horse nearby, but of course the animal could have run off into the storm.

Clay soon discovered the man had a bullet hole in his chest and blood was making the shirt sticky. He felt grimly for a heart-beat and decided the man was not dead; but with a wound like that it was only a matter of time. There was little he could do for the man beyond propping him up so that he did not choke on his own blood.

The range man opened pain-filled eyes. In a moment of lucidity he evidently saw Clay clearly and began to mutter hoarse, spasmodic words.

"Fogel . . . shot me . . . taken my gold . . . "

The man coughed and almost choked and his words ceased. Then: "Fogel . . . rode with me . . . down the trail . . . said he was going to Waco . . . "

"Yes?" Clay could only prompt the man.

"Said . . . he was going to join up . . . with the big boss in Waco . . . ah . . . ah!"

And that was all Clay heard for the man went limp with strange suddenness. Clay knew he had died.

He laid the guy down, grim, feeling it was a lousy thing to die like this. As a deputy he had seen sudden death many times but the experience always left a sad feeling in the heart. A man had died: what kind of man, he did not know; he was just dead.

There was little Clay could do in this buffeting storm. He could not bury him: it was spooking the horse and the animal needed a firm grip. Clay put a foot in a stirrup and swung to saddle leather. Urging the horse on, he scrutinised the surrounding terrain with eyes that felt raw with the scouring sand.

The man's words were firmly planted in his mind. A galoot named Fogel — a killer: there was no one in Waco that Clay knew by the name.

But this unknown had killed and taken the guy's gold. It seemed the dead feller had been a miner, maybe a placer miner panning gold, although the trail the man had been pursuing was a long way from the Rio Pecos river, where the valuable dust was found.

So the man called Fogel had ridden

along with this miner and then shot him. Greed for gold was a deadly thing. And this Fogel character intended to join up with the big boss in Waco.

Now who the hell was this big boss?

Discovering this man's identity would be an exciting thing, for this was the person who had employed Rolf Lester and Seth Mundy and others around the Waco territory. A mystery man, indeed. There wasn't a clue as to his personality, let alone a description.

The man hired others, that was an obvious point. Seemingly he didn't ride with his hired rogues. There wasn't a whisper anywhere about the man being seen with the hellions he hired. This unknown boss had hired the gun-hands whom Clay had killed out in the wastelands when the gold had been driven out by buckboard. Gold! It seemed the big boss was partial to gold, bullion or raw metal. The same unknown had paid the gun-happy hombres to shoot up the sheriff's office.

He was behind a great deal of lawless activity and yet he contrived to be an unknown. But some must know him. Someone could talk — if that chance presented itself. And apparently the boss man was about to receive a new ally in the man called Fogel. Clay made a mental note to look at new faces in Waco.

The slow ride back to town was a struggle against the elements, the horse tiring and showing signs of panic when a fresh gust of sand-filled air hit it. But man and animal made it finally. When Clay rode slowly down the main stem, awnings were flapping and torn under the wind pressure. No other men were on the streets. Sand in the eyes and mouth wasn't something people sought.

Clay reached the sheriff's office. He walked the game horse into the cover of the livery and left the animal there, still saddled. He wanted to see the sheriff. He did pause to beat dust out of his range clothes and his hat. He felt as dry as the inside of a chimney. A good long drink was indicated. Clay could not find him in the office, so he left again, locking the door.

He was a young man and no solitary hombre: he liked to find his friends in a saloon just like any other man. He went along to the Bonanza Saloon. He thought he might see Jesse Teed or old Doc Hawton, and even the latter's humourless conversation might be appreciated after the ride through the storm. But a long drink would be best. As to the Doc, well at least he was no killer or gun-happy ruffian. He might come across Hoot Sampson. The sheriff should be somewhere unless he was interviewing somebody.

Clay immediately saw Doc Hawton when he went through the batwings. The man was fond of a glass of rye although he was never drunk. "Howdy, Doc."

The other turned. "Hello, young man. I see you are seeking shelter from the sand-storm."

"Reckon it's blowing out now — after I've battled through it."

"You were out in this blow? You're a son-of-a-bitch for duty!"

"Yeah. I rode through it, coming down from the Circle Four. Found a dying man on the trail, Doc."

"Another body. This town will soon be one large boothill."

Clay laughed. "Have a drink with me. It ain't as bad as all that. Always plenty of decent folks in any town. It's the bad hombres who make the most noise and trouble. Don't you figure Waco is a mighty fine town? Going to be important if it keeps on growing."

At that moment Dave Lansing walked up to them, immaculate in a brown serge suit, a watch-chain across the thick waistcoat although the air was warm in the saloon. "Hello, gents! See you figure the Bonanza is the safest place in town when a blow is on."

"One saloon is the same as others to me," declared Clay.

"Is that so? Wal, I don't figure that

100

at all, Deputy. The Bonanza is the finest place in Waco, better than the Gold Nugget or the Last Chance. See they got a new manager at the Last Chance. Seems this galoot just rode in — through that goldarned storm — and took over."

Doc Hawton glanced up. He was much smaller than Lansing. "A new citizen?" he inquired in his studious tones.

"Is that was you'd call him?" Dave Lansing laughed. "I heard his name was Fogel."

The name tensed Clay's interest. "How come this stranger got the job?"

"You're asking me somethin' I know nothing about. All I heard was the gent rode into town with the storm at its height — which makes him a tough galoot, I'd say. Reckon he had it arranged, with papers of introduction because Winters, the old manager, was ready to hand over. Old Winters is going to live with his married daughter on her ranch."

Clay was thoughtful. "Reckon I'll wander along to the Last Chance and introduce myself. You coming, Doc?"

"Not until this storm is completely clear, Deputy. No, sir. Sand in the throat can cause many bodily ills."

"Reckon I'll go along just the same," and Clay grinned at the old Doc and left him with Dave Lansing.

As he shouldered through the rough wind outside, he fell to pondering Dave Lansing. He had suspected him of being the boss who hired Rolf Lester and other law-challenging toughies, and of engineering the railroad holdups. Hoot Sampson had held that opinion but had always said; 'Ain't an atom of proof. We're just talkin' hunches — and that ain't good enough, Clay. And maybe we're wrong, huh?'

"Yeah, maybe. This boss hides his identity well . . . "

Dave Lansing had been ready to provide Rolf and Seth with alibis the night they had ridden out into the wastelands. Why? Why had he stuck his neck out, with words that were obvious lies?

The dying man had said Fogel was going to join the 'big boss' in Waco, but those words could be interpreted many ways. The 'big boss' could be another big boss, or the words could be just loose talk. On the other hand with lawless men the big boss would surely be the unknown organiser of banditry. But if this man, Fogel, had taken over the managership of the Last Chance Saloon, how did that tie in? Who owned the Last Chance?"

Clay wondered if Dave Lansing really owned the Last Chance. It would be a good idea to make some inquiries.

Clay made his way down the road and found the Last Chance batwings. The storm was playing out; the wind less intense — but a man had to hold on to his hat! And he could walk upright without leaning on the wind now.

He entered the saloon and moved up to the counter. Due to the storm, the place was pretty full. Men in range garb propped up the mahogany counter and argued and drank. Clay spotted two hard galoots, gun-packers, but they were boozed and not looking for fights. No one took much notice of the dusty deputy.

He soon located Fogel. The man was behind the bar, studying some ledgers. His perusal was pretty perfunctory, for he suddenly pushed them to one side with a cynical laugh as if he didn't care.

He was a big guy, in dust-covered riding clothes. Whatever his past history or occupations, he was certainly not a saloon manager. He did not look the part and he did not have the pot-belly associated with men who spent a lot of time serving drink. The man's black shirt, dusty now, rippled with the big body inside. He wore a large Stetson even in the saloon, behind the bar, which wasn't customary with drink slingers. More significant, he had two Colts, identical butts, clung on his thighs and they were there for use. He wasn't some guy out of a Cody circus. He was wearing leather riding chaps which had seen a lot of miles on horse-back.

Clay studied the man without betraying too much interest. Unless the dying man had been crazy, Fogel had shot him cold-bloodedly and made off with his gold. A killer breed, with two guns backing up that assessment.

Fogel had a bold sort of face, with dark amused eyes and a permanent cynical smile. A beard stubble covered his chin but Clay had the feeling the man clean-shaved when not riding the trails.

A dangerous hombre, was Clay's mental summing-up.

Fogel was not attracting much attention in the saloon. Maybe the customers had looked at him and accepted him. The bartender was showing the man some of the stock of bottles. Then Clay heard the bartender call Fogel 'Bert' once or twice. So that was his full name, apparently.

Maybe a look at the wanted posters in the sheriffs office might provide a clue. He came out of the Last Chance Saloon and thrust through the dying storm winds until he reached the office.

He spent an hour looking at old records of wanted men but none matched up with the appearance of this Bert Fogel. Then Clay turned to Hoot Sampson who was in another room slowly writing out some details of a case into a book. Hoot's writing ability was of the laborious kind. He was more capable with men, horses and cattle than the quill.

"I've been looking at the new manager of the Last Chance," Clay announced.

"Yeah? What's he done?"

"Wal, he killed a galoot out on the trail and took his gold . . . "

Hoot raised bushy eyebrows. Red as his moustache, they gave him a fierce appearance — which wasn't always appropriate.

"You ain't joking, huh? I ain't heard of the feller."

"Reckon he's the latest addition to Waco's gun-happy rannies."

Hoot stopped writing. "How come you know this?"

"Wal, I was riding through the storm — I'd been over to the Circle Four — "

"Not again, Clay, huh?" Hoot was amused.

"Yeah. In the storm I heard a shot. Thought at first it was all in my mind. But I found this dying man. Reckon he was a miner — wasn't any other clue. He muttered something about a man called Fogel had robbed him and shot him and left him for dead, which was about right because he did die right there on my hands. But before he gave his last breath, he told me that this Fogel hombre was going to join up with the big boss in Waco."

"You don't say!" Hoot Sampson glared. "The big boss, whoever the hell he is!"

"So I find this Bert Fogel taking over

the Last Chance. He apparently ain't buying into the joint. He's the new manager. Say, Hoot, do you know who actually owns the Last Chance?"

The other man fingered his bristly moustache and muttered: "Now that you ask I can't rightly say that I know who owns the property. Old Winters has been the manager for some time."

"He's leaving . . . "

"Yeah — I heard. Maybe Dave Lansing owns the place."

"You think?"

"Wal, he's got fingers in many pies."

"Reckon I'll have to do some investigating. Because maybe the hombre who owns the Last Chance is the big boss behind these robberies."

"Yep, Clay, you do that an' earn your salary an' make our councilmen happy. You might get the information over at the County Building. They got all records of land and property in this town."

Clay nodded. He had become

determined to find out who owned the Last Chance Saloon now that this man Bert Fogel was on the scene. It might be a false alarm or a small point that had no real value, but he would look into it.

5

BECAUSE it was not a matter for haste, and because he wanted to eat and wash some of the sand out of his ears and so on, Clay waited until the wind dropped to normal. Like most storms from the direction of the wastelands, it reached a peak and then quickly subsided. Then he set off for the County Building.

He went slowly down the main stem on foot, noting the drifts of sand and grit. Already men and women were busy cleaning up, shovelling the unwanted sand to vacant plots, clearing porches and doorways. The sun blazed down, an orange-red globe. The rest of the day, what was left of it, would be hot until sundown.

He entered the County Building and saw a clerk who got him the relevant records of land claims and property assessments, Clay quickly traced through the columns of inked records, all in fine copper-plate. He quickly got to know who owned the Last Chance Saloon. Malcolm Starn.

Thoughtfully, Clay left the building.

He wondered why Malcolm Starn should employ a man like Bert Fogel who didn't seem to fit any description of a saloon keeper. He wondered what sort of situation had arisen that enabled a man to ride in from unknown parts and take over the managership of the saloon, for Bert Fogel was obviously a gun-hand pure and simple. Of course, there were factors behind all this which were at present a mystery.

If the dying miner was to be believed, Fogel was joining up with the unknown big boss in Waco. But in reality this Fogel had just taken up a job in the saloon, something that must have been arranged some time ago. How long had Malcolm Starn known Fogel? And why employ him? It seemed a mix-up situation which no doubt someone could explain, that someone obviously Malcolm Starn — or this Bert Fogel hombre.

Clay expelled breath impatiently. He much preferred action to speculation. He discarded the notion of going along to Starn and asking him about Fogel. If Starn had anything to hide he certainly would not reveal it in answer to a few questions.

Clay had a hunch that it would be better to leave the situation to simmer until answers were brewed in the melting pot. But he would give Hoot Sampson the results of his small attempts at investigation.

"That feller Starn has his finger in all sorts of enterprises," growled the sheriff, after Clay had given him the facts. "He's pretty shrewd, but I can't figure out why he should hire this Fogel galoot. As you say, he don't seem a regular saloon-keeper."

"Give them a bit of rope," suggested Clay.

"Yeah, often hangs a guy . . ."

"I'm not forgetting that Fogel killed a man, and I'm going out to get the cadaver. There's a slug in it, maybe more than one. A slug is a mighty good bit of evidence."

"Yep. If you can find the hogleg that fired it, Clay."

The young deputy was as good as his word. With a fresh horse and some determination he rode out of Waco and an easy life, down the trail that led to the Circle Four.

He inevitably thought about Mary Lester. He was always thinking about her, in fact, with her lovely smile always in his mind, the way she could laugh at his jokes. Although of late there had been little in her life in which to find amusement, thanks to her troublesome brothers, Tad and Rolf.

Mary should have a better life. She would make a good wife. In a way he regretted being a lawman, because he'd had to kill Tad and fight with Rolf, although the latter was pure enmity and not based on any rule of law.

But he had a grim feeling that that would come and Rolf would have to answer for some crime.

The killing of the unknown miner had taken place a few miles from the Circle Four ranch, which was some sort of location but not very definite because of the sand-storm. It wouldn't be easy to pin-point the exact spot.

He rode around for a long time, standing in the stirrups, staring at the landscape, noting some distant cattle. It was the buzzards that finally helped him. Seeing them slowly circling, he galloped up at speed and angrily scattered the scavengers.

The body was partly covered by drifting sand, which had saved it from the buzzards. Sand was everywhere but in a few weeks, if there was rain, it would sink into the earth and the grass would grow.

The vultures wheeled overhead as if reluctant to depart. Clay pulled the body to one side and then heaved it over his horse. He mounted behind.

For a moment he wished he could see Mary Lester but decided he had not time for this luxury. He began to ride back to Waco with the sun declining on the horizon. He decided a bit grimly he was weary of horse-flesh and saddle-leather.

As he entered the town much later, the horse slowed with the double burden, there were Mexican children and chickens still playing in the dust outside shacks in the poorer area and a few men stared at the deputy riding with the dead man.

Clay got Doc Hawton to come along to the sheriff's office and do a bit of surgery in extracting the bullet. It might be a good idea to have Doc Hawton as a witness that this slug had been taken from the dead man, if there was any way later of identifying the slug. The man would have to be buried. Plenty quick, Clay decided with a grimace at the stench. It was too hot for dead bodies in Waco just now.

The slug was a .44 fired from a

long-barrelled Colt. Not the usual Colt ammunition. "One or two scratches on this slug," muttered Clay as he examined the metal with a magnifying glass. "We might prove that it came out of Bert Fogel's twin Colts if we ever get the chance to look closely at that galoot's hardware."

The grave-digger was sent for and the body taken to boothill. Maybe someone would say a few words over the body. It wasn't Clay's duty to fix that. Like most rough-living illiterate miners there was no document on the body to make identification possible. He was just one more dead man.

Clay and Hoot Sampson, as single men, were having a meal in the Chinese-run eating-house a bit later. Chores were over, or so they figured: the dead man had been disposed of, and that was all anyone could say about the poor devil. The heat of the day had vanished and sundown would come quickly as it did in these parts.

They were barely through their jerky

beef and beans when a rider careered up the main stem, startling hitched animals, and leaping from his mount and rushing into the restaurant.

"Heard you were here, Sheriff," he bawled. "There's been a holdup over at the Dorado Gold Company place, down at the Rio Pecos river. They want you there — "

"Oh, do they?" roared Hoot Sampson. "Can't you see I'm eating?"

"Hell, it's important!"

"So is eating!"

Clay smiled. "Are we going, Hoot? I mean, what's the blamed hurry? They'll be miles away . . . "

The rider was a hired hand from the gold company and his name was Sam Jansen. He talked, watching Hoot and Clay eat, as if they had no right to take it easy. "Ain't we going? Hell, I've ridden all this way — "

"You're under orders. You'd be fired if you didn't. Does your boss figure we can work miracles? We can't fly across that damned terrain."

Clay grinned. "Some day, you know, men will fly . . . "

"Don't talk shit," growled Hoot Sampson. "We'll never have wings."

"I was reading — "

"Guess you read too much, young feller." And the sheriff shovelled more grub into a large mouth and winked at Sam Jansen.

"I read this account in a newspaper from the east about this man who built a flying machine outa wood with wings that flapped up and down like an eagle's . . . "

"Hell, are you going loco! Aw, damn — guess we'll get some fresh mounts and ride again."

"I've spent a helluva lot of time in the saddle today," began Clay.

"You sure have. The councilmen will give you a medal. An' talking about councilmen maybe they'll cut down on the limits we gotta operate out of Waco. The Dorado Gold Company shouldn't be in our jurisdiction." Hoot Sampson was working up a fine indignation over the local politics, something he enjoyed at intervals.

They got some account of the holdup from Sam Jansen. "Three fellers just rode in and grabbed bags of dust. They was wearing masks. Couldn't see nothin'. Big galoots, it seems."

"Did you see 'em?"

"No, but that's what I was told."

"They're always big galoots, these baddies," grunted Hoot. "According to the folks who actually see 'em. Maybe that's the excuse for not doing anything."

"They just rode in," said Sam Jansen. "They kilt one man who figured to shoot at 'em. They grabbed the bags of gold outa the assaying office. Must ha' known what to find."

"Did no one get an idea who the cusses were?" shouted the sheriff.

"Nope. Might have been any galoot. Hats pulled down over their danged eyes. I seen them riding out. Three men from the gold company set off after them. One guy was the manager."

"Maybe they caught up with the hellions?"

"Nope. That's what we all figured but only two men came riding back. Them robbers had shot one man — one of the guards we got. That's when I set off for town."

"Wal, those smart operators sure got plenty of start," grumbled the sheriff. "All we can do now is aim to pick up their sign."

Clay nodded. He knew they were too late to get within shooting distance of the robbers. Time and distance were on the side of the rogues.

Delay was inevitable. They had to get fresh horses and saddle them. They had to grab at grub bags and water bottles, in case they were out in the wilds for any length of time. So after an interval the two lawmen and Sam Jansen were riding out again, two lawmen grimly sick of the time spent in the saddle recently.

They went steadily in the direction of the Rio Pecos, towards the canyon in which the Dorado Gold Company operated.

Clay privately thought that Hoot was right about the limits of their jurisdiction as Waco law officers. There was enough to concern them within the town boundaries and nearby. But the councilmen had set these limits long ago when Waco was a small place, and this was before Hoot Sampson's time.

Hoofs pounded the semi-arid land. The aroma of sage floated through the air. Hours later, as in silence they neared the vast canyon, they found the cholla and ocotillo and other desert growths increasingly numerous, indicating the wasteland conditions. These vegetations were interspersed with the towering saguaros, monstrous cacti.

Then the three riders turned sweating mounts into the canyon which lay parallel with the rock-bound Rio Pecos river. Here mesquite and grama grass grew in tufts, of sustenance to cattle; but no one ran steers in this area.

Instead, the log buildings of the Dorado Gold Company squatted on the sand, shale and grass. The buildings were stout, made from logs which had been floated down the river from the distant hills where the trees grew.

As the three riders rode slowly into the yard around the mine workings, two men with horses came towards them.

"We're riding out with you," declared John Filby, the mine manager. The other burly man was a hired guard, with a Colt in a frayed leather holster, a shotgun in his saddle holster. He had a tight, unsmiling countenance, as if grimness was part of his everyday experience.

"Hold it," snapped Hoot Sampson. "You ain't going to catch up with them villains. They're gone to hell by now."

"Yeah, but you're gonna get them, ain't you?"

The sheriff waved a hand to the surrounding land. "This is a helluva big land. Maybe we can track 'em, maybe not."

"Maybe we need new lawmen," sneered the other.

"Maybe!" bawled the sheriff in anger. "You can have my job, friend, if you're interested. Or maybe diggin' gold out of these rocks is more lucrative!"

Sam Jansen, Clay, the sheriff and John Filby all glared at each other. And then, as Hoot Sampson took a swig at his water bottle, tempers subsided. "Gold and hellions — they go together," growled the sheriff.

"I'm going to my bunk," stated Sam Jansen. "I done enough."

The hired guard with John Filby looked expectantly at his boss. He nodded and shot a glance at Hoot Sampson. The sheriff nodded reluctantly and growled. "All right, let's go. What the hell! We'll scour a few miles. It ain't gonna do any good."

The four horsemen urged horses off into a cloud of dust, heading down the canyon. Clay privately thought that the sheriff was right. The robbers would be to hell and hide out of it by now. Still, they had to do something.

"Those hell-bents shot one of our men," shouted John Filby. "The cusses plugged him in the guts and he was losing so much blood we had to turn back with him to save his life."

"And they killed one feller at the start, too," commented Clay. "That makes 'em right nice gents."

John Filby was able to take them right out into the desert to the spot where they had turned back with the badly-wounded guard. The robbers' trail showed clear ahead, with fresh hoof marks dug deep into the sand. Where the land was shale there were clear indications that hoofs had kicked aside the yellow flat stones. It was like this for a long way ahead: endless wasteland.

Clay exchanged glances with Hoot Sampson, grim glances. John Filby rode with the hired guard and once or twice they rode off at a tangent on the wrong trail marks.

"Thisaway!" snarled Hoot Sampson, pointing at the right trail signs made by the robbers.

"Sure?" inquired John Filby.

"Sure I'm sure!" A fresh snarl from the angry sheriff.

In truth, Hoot Sampson was an experienced hand at reading sign. He'd been taught years ago by Indians.

As the miles went by and they followed the sign, Clay and the sheriff realised the robbers had ridden for Pueblo, a Mexican town just over the border. This was the place, just over forty years ago, where Santa Anna and the Mexicans had scored great victories at Buena Vista and Palo Alto.

"Once they get into that hell-town, how can I get 'em out?" grumbled the sheriff to Clay as they rode side by side.

The deputy nodded. "No way."

Clay knew the Mexican town was simply a rendezvous for every lawless hombre on the run for a hundred miles around and more. There was another point, too, which was the fact that Hoot Sampson had no authority over the border. Pueblo was decidedly out of his bailiwick.

"Good mind to call it a day," said Hoot.

John Filby caught the shouted remark. "What about our gold?"

"What about it?" sneered the sheriff. "Reckon you'd better dig for more! Aw, hell — there ain't even any kind of lawman in this stinking burg who I could call on and leave the job there."

Nevertheless, they rode into the adobe buildings of the ramshackle town about an hour later, tired men on equally tired animals, sweat-flecked and needing water. No person of any respectability lived in Pueblo. Hoot Sampson was seething, knowing the ride was a waste of his time and only the obstinacy of John Filby had brought them to this point.

Naked children played happily in the

alkali dust, with dogs and chickens, and men in steeply shaped hats lounged and sprawled in the shade of a few wooden porches.

"Sure stinks," growled Hoot.

The party rode slowly down the main stem, past some adobe cantinas where bars consisted of a few planks across two barrels, and fat frowsy women eyed any passerby with speculative interest.

Finally the sheriff halted the whole thing. "Wal, we've lost those robbing hombres, Filby. Satisfied?"

The sheriff leaned heavily on his saddle horn and wiped the sweat and dust from his face with a red kerchief. John Filby glared futilely around him. "I swear those hellions we've just passed weren't greasers. Those three men — you saw 'em — they were white!"

"Hell, you ain't been here before!" snapped the sheriff.

"You'll find a few white renegades in this dump," Clay pointed out.

"Yeah — worse hell-bents than the

greasers!" The sheriff spat.

It was rather amazing, one of life's little ironies, but even as Hoot spoke up the blistered batwing doors of a nearby cantina swung and three men walked out on to the dirt road. They moved slowly, even lazily, with insolence written all over them, and even as they moved they were making brown-paper cigarettes and preparing to light them.

The three dusty men were enjoying their sneering appearance. Clay Mandell found himself staring at Rolf and Seth Mundy. The third guy was more than interesting.

Bert Fogel casually lit his cigarette as if the sheriff of Waco and his men did not exist.

"Wal, I'm damned!" Hoot Sampson growled. "You gents have sure done a helluva lot of riding!"

The sheriff was out of his saddle before he realised afresh that this town was not within his jurisdiction. But that did not deter Hoot from speaking his mind.

"I ain't going to bandy words with you jiggers! I reckon you just rode into town in the last hour. I figure you're the hard cases who robbed the Dorado Gold Company. I can't prove it, but by Gawd I'll remember it!"

"Arrest these men, Sheriff!" snapped John Filby.

Hoot Sampson ignored the man.

"You lot going loco with the heat an' too much saddle-sweat?" sneered Rolf Lester. "We don't know what the hell you're talkin' about!"

"This is Mexico, Sheriff," grated Seth Mundy. "An' we've been here all day! Heh! Heh!"

"What doing?"

"Aw, just drinking."

"You'd be topped to your blasted hat if you'd been here all day drinking this rot-gut," snapped the sheriff.

"Have you been here long, Fogel?" Clay asked quietly.

He knew he would not get a straight answer, but there would be some grim amusement in extracting a reply from the two-gun man.

"Nope. I just rode in and met up with these gents. I'm new to these parts . . . "

"Sure. You've taken over the Last Chance Saloon. You like that kind of business?"

"Yeah, I like it," drawled the man and there was amusement in his dark eyes.

"Do you know anything about the robbery?"

"Not a blasted thing, Deputy. You figure I look like a robber?"

Fogel's hands hovered above his Colt butts. Clay thinned his lips, staring back, trying to read the guy's mind. He knew Fogel would not be fool enough to go for gun-play. Survival did not depend on it. He had nothing to gain, and when bullets started flying even a clever rannigan could lose out.

But the man was certainly a robber. For a start, he had killed the man in the sandstorm and robbed him of his gold. Now he had apparently linked up with Rolf Lester. And hadn't the dying miner said Fogel intended to meet up with the big boss? Rolf and Seth were in the pay of this boss. And gold in one shape or another seemed to be the main lure. Maybe the management of the Last Chance Saloon was just a front.

Hoot Sampson got to his horse again. "Let's get. We can't pin anythin' on these jiggers — an' they know it!"

"By thunder," began John Filby, "they kill a man and you just want to ride out!"

"We'll get them in the act some day," rapped Hoot. "Then they'll get plumb riddled with lead."

"In the meantime they get free."

"Allus another day," growled Hoot.

The horsemen rode slowly back through the smelly dust of the main street, a few indolent characters sitting in rockers on porches watching them with sleepy interest or suspicion, mostly the latter.

"That Fogel guy is just another

gunman," muttered Hoot as he and Clay rode stirrup to stirrup. "You don't have to tell me what he is. I can see his ornery character plenty plain."

"I don't get the tie-up with Malcolm Starn."

"Nope. Pretty odd, that."

"Starn must know something about this feller," mused Clay. "He knows the kind of man he is employing."

"Durned fast mover, too." Hoot took his hat off and fanned his face. "He ain't been in this territory more than a few hours an he kills a galoot and takes his gold. Then he fixes up with Rolf Lester and helps to rob the Dorado Gold Company."

Clay nodded. "The big boss is behind it." Clay fell to thinking about Mary, prompted by the thought that her brother was so involved in this lawlessness. There seemed no way he could protect her. Some day she'd suffer more anguish because of her brothers, Tad and Rolf, because some day Rolf would face punishment.

Clay halted his nag. "Look, I've got an idea I'd like to play. I'm riding back into Pueblo."

"What in hell are you up to?"

"I got a hunch I can play — alone. You ride back to Waco."

"I'll play this hunch with you."

"Nope. You've done enough ridin' for one day."

"And so the heck have you, young feller!" roared Hoot.

"That's just it. I'm a young feller."

Clay wheeled his horse and applied spurs. The animal crow-hopped at first in alarm and then went off fast and Clay waved a hand as he departed. He went back into the ramshackle border town.

He was sometimes impulsive and as Hoot had indicated he was young, and this mixture had sent him back to investigate. Sure, he was fed-up with sweat and dust and horse-flesh but he just wanted to get near to Rolf Lester, Bert Fogel and the odious Seth. Clay's hunch centred around Bert Fogel's guns. One of those big, low-slung Colts had killed the unknown miner. The slug from the miner's body had not hit a bone and had not spread. It could be proved to have been fired from one of Fogel's guns, with new ideas about barrel scoring, if they could get the right gun for examination.

That was his hunch. He realised it was a way-out idea.

He rode back into the first few adobes and shacks and then hitched his horse to a tie-rail at the back of a yard. He walked slowly, with long strides, slow because of the time he'd had in the saddle, and he passed Mexicans lying on plank walks in shady corners. There were a few frowsy senoritas beside the shacks and single-roomed adobe houses, and one waved invitingly. He passed children sitting in holes in the roadway where there were chickens, dogs and goats. There was not much activity except a woman singing a wailing Border song.

Clay approached the cantina where

he had last seen Rolf Lester and Bert Fogel. He stopped in some shade and watched the dirty white building where he could see three horses tied to a hitching-rail. He recognised the big roan as belonging to the Lester remuda. The other two animals were wiry ponies such as were used a lot on ranches. It was a cert these were not Mexican animals.

Even as Clay hung around, unsure for the moment, eyeing events, a rider cantered his mount around a corner building in the road and came down to the other three horses at the tie-rail.

The man dismounted, threw the leathers around the rail and walked stiffly into the adobe cantina.

He was a medium-sized man wearing a store suit. The black serge was powdered with trail dust. He was a Waco man and Clay knew him well.

The man was Malcolm Starn.

6

CLAY figured it was time he took a look into the cantina, and so he walked swiftly across the road and approached the sun-blistered bat-wing doors. He stopped there, taut, listening.

He took a look into the dim interior, where he could hear voices. As his eyes became accustomed to the comparative darkness within, he saw Malcolm Starn standing in social sympathy with the three other men. Raucous laughter proved the men were well regaled with some drink. In fact, Rolf Lester and his two cronies seemed to be enjoying some joke. He walked in suddenly, lithe strides taking him to the rough plank counter before the others were aware of him.

He looked at them steadily, grimly, and the laughter ceased.

"Howdy, Mister Starn!" Clay greeted the man deliberately.

The man seemed to stiffen in every muscle and his lean smallish face seemed to be suddenly lined and set and very wary. "Howdy, Deputy."

The half-breed bartender moved up, stared at Clay, a frowsy moustache nearly into his mouth.

"Red eye," said Clay and he smiled at Starn. "You drinking?"

"No. I — I — don't care for liquor at this moment."

"Wal, I ain't asking your pals," declared Clay.

When the bartender placed the drink in front of him, he swiftly drank it and felt he needed it.

Rolf Lester shot an amused glance at Bert Fogel, a look that Clay intercepted. He gathered that Rolf had taken a fancy to Bert Fogel in that they were birds of a feather although Fogel was the more dangerous ruffian. Rolf Lester simply had the conceit and red guts of a wild young rannigan.

"I thought you'd headed back to Waco, Deputy?" Rolf Lester felt the need to taunt. There was more than that in his piercing gaze. Clay knew he was itching to start some rough play.

"Don't think," advised Clay. "It can lead to mistakes and hurt your brain — as well as other parts of your anatomy. For instance, I figured you and your pals robbed the gold company and shot two men: but thinking ain't proving." Clay turned to Starn, stared into his set face and said: "You heard about the robbery at the gold company?"

Starn nodded. "Sure. I heard before I rode out."

"I figure these rannigans did it." And Clay waved a hand at the other three.

But he was watching for sign of emotion on Starn's visage. The freight-line owner showed no response to his verbal probe, no surprise. Taut lines etched deeply into the man's face as he maintained his poker mask.

Rolf Lester's rough laugh suddenly

138

rang through the empty cantina. "As you said, Deputy, thinking ain't provin'. I reckon you are boring Mister Starn and I don't like you boring my pals. Time we livened things up a bit, huh?"

It had been Clay Mandell's intention to gain a hint as to why Malcolm Starn had travelled into Pueblo. Clay got the message that Starn had known where to find Rolf Lester and the others. The whole setup was very dubious and Starn's face gave nothing away and his words even less.

Suddenly Rolf Lester whipped his hardware from the shiny holster. He pointed the gun at Clay's boots and the weapon barked. Slugs tore into the planks. Gunsmoke hazed up in front of Clay's eyes and nostrils. Rolf Lester triggered as fast as any man could do. "Dance, you nosy bastard!"

Clay never moved.

His boots stood square and flat on the boards and as the slugs bit into the rough wood he did not move a muscle.

It was, of course, an ordeal and the only help he had was in knowing he'd seen this trick performed on others.

His hands hung by his side, one set of fingers only an inch from his gun butt. The slugs tore splinters out of the wood, embedding deeply, with gunsmoke rising like an acrid cloud. Then the gun was empty and Clay had not taken his eyes off the other man's sneer-twisted features.

The moment Rolf Lester's gun was empty Clay whipped his six-gun from the leather, scooping with real speed, and the weapon pointed at the men, ready to whip to any one individual. Fogel and Seth Mundy were beaten on the draw, Bert Fogel's hands stopping inches from his gun-butts. Wise in the ways of guns and men, he knew that one false move, even a twitchy finger, and he was dead. As for the seedy Seth, he was numbed. Challenges were not to his liking. A sneaky shot from out of the dark was his idea of an encounter.

"Now Mister Starn, you can help the law," snapped Clay. "Rolf has had his fun. Take the hoglegs out of the leathers, Mister Starn, and I mean all of them — everybody. And if you happen to pack a little hidden Derringer you can include that, too. Any tricks and some jigger ends up dead."

"I assure you I have no gun, Deputy," muttered the man. "And I want to help the law. I believe in the law . . . "

"Wal, get the guns."

Clay had his eyes on Bert Fogel's pearl-inlaid Colts. This was the opportunity he wanted. He wanted those twin Colts, for reasons maybe the others did not suspect.

The frozen tableau was interrupted when the half-breed bartender behind the plank counter decided in a foolish moment to oppose the man with the law badge. It might have been his instinct but it was a fool idea.

The 'breed clumsily moved out a

shotgun from behind part of the rough counter. The weapon was heavy and he was slow, a terrible combination for Clay did not risk anything. As the fool of a man made his silly play, without a chance of winning, Clay triggered.

Admittedly, he was on edge, every nerve taut, and it was his only way to react. Clay's Colt flared flame, smoke and bullet. The slug hit the 'breed between the eyes and he fell back like a sack of spuds, the shotgun clattering to the floor, unfired.

Fogel did jerk — but Clay's gun swung to him even as the Colt-smoke still filtered from the gun.

"Don't do it — or you're dead!"

The tableau settled again. Clay gestured to Malcolm Starn. "Get collecting the hardware like I told you."

The freight-line owner, pulling guns out of holsters and backing carefully each time, as if the men concerned might grab at him or a gun, threw the weapons onto a nearby table. Clay faced furious men, his Colt keeping them at bay.

Clay was not sure of Malcolm Starn any more. The facts were that the man was employing Bert Fogel as manager of the Last Chance, and he had ridden into the Mexican town to meet up with the gunman. Was Starn behind the robbery of the gold company? It seemed a bit incredible — but what were the answers?

Starn finished collecting the guns. Clay moved carefully, his gun still a menace to the angry men. Clay picked up Fogel's pearl-studded Colts and held them in one capable hand.

Blood trickled across the rough floor from the corpse lying behind the bar.

"Mighty fine work, Mister Starn. Now if we could only get the gold these rogues took out of the gold company's offices, we'd sure pin murder on them."

"You ain't got a hell's chance of pinning that on us," snarled Rolf Lester. "You won't find no gold!"

He had found plenty of pleasure in

143

trying to make Clay Mandell dance in fear but he saw no humour in the present situation.

"Reckon you must have been met by some rider," snapped Clay. "You ain't foolin' no one. Three fellers robbed the gold company and killed one man and badly wounded another. Them jiggers headed this way. We ride up and find you lot here. It sure adds up to a lot of sneaky doings."

"Just your suspicious mind, Deputy," drawled Bert Fogel.

"Yep. I got a suspicious mind where you're concerned, feller. But I'm working on them suspicions, don't worry. Hoot Sampson an' me will keep on working until some of you galoots are either dead or behind bars."

"The hell with you!"

"Adios, amigos. Enjoy Pueblo's rotgut while you got the chance. I'm going. Coming, Mister Starn? Or have you got further business with these hell-bent gents?"

"I'll come with you."

"Wal, get those hoglegs. I don't want a slug in the back. We can drop these guns down the road. It'll give these men something to do picking them up."

Clay did not tell Bert Fogel that his guns would be examined under a magnifying glass.

The freight-line owner reluctantly gathered the hardware and left the cantina with Clay. Malcolm Starn got to his saddle and rode down Pueblo's apology for a main street to where Clay had tethered his horse. The three men watched them from the cantina with grim, displeased stares.

Clay Mandell and Starn rode out into the arid lands in silence, Starn holding the confiscated guns. Clay did not fear the man and after a while he turned to him. "You can throw them irons into the dust now, Mister Starn. Maybe them hombres will ride out in search for the hardware, maybe not. I don't kinda care much."

Starn hurriedly threw the guns

near some catclaw and then glanced questioningly at the pearl-handled weapons. "You keeping them?"

"Yeah. I've got reasons. These shooters are .44 barrelled. Ain't so many of them around. Mostly .45."

He did not inform the other man that he was trying to prove that Fogel's guns had fired the bullet that had killed the unknown miner. The slugs that had killed and wounded the men in the robbery of the Dorado Gold Company would be .45 and it would be almost impossible to prove that Rolf Lester or Seth Mundy had killed those men. .45 Colts were so numerous that nothing could be deduced from proving that a .45 piece of lead had killed the gold company employees. But maybe it was possible to trace the few owners of .44 weapons in Waco. The killing might be narrowed down to Fogel. It was just a slight chance. Maybe the man would stop some lead himself in a vital part before these technicalities were put into effect.

"Those guns are Fogel's," said Malcolm Starn, very carefully.

"Yeah?"

"You know that man is working for me now, Mandell?"

"Yeah. How come you hired him?"

"I wanted a strong hand for the Last Chance. The saloon is getting kinda lawless. I'm a firm believer in law and order, Deputy."

"Yeah. You keep on telling me." Clay wondered why Starn was so insistent upon his love of law and order.

"How much did you know about Fogel when you hired him?"

"He was recommended to me. The other manager wanted to retire, and business wasn't so good under him."

Clay nodded. He noted the other man had provided an answer in every point. Was Starn a bit too ready with answers?

"If Bert Fogel is working for you, Mister Starn, I ought to tell you he's a bad hombre."

"Maybe. But that's just your opinion, Deputy."

"He's hard and a killer. I am keeping an eye on him; and so is Hoot Sampson."

Starn nodded. "I'll bear your comments in mind and keep an eye on Bert Fogel."

Clay sat tall in the saddle for a moment, staring at the distant horizon over the hard-baked sand. They were descending a shale incline, alone in the silent land where only rattlers hid.

"Maybe you can tell me why you rode over to Pueblo — that miserable excuse for a town — to see those other hell-bents?"

"I just went that way," snapped the other.

"You knew they'd be there."

"I knew Fogel would be there. I only wanted to see him."

"Business?"

"Yep. Business, Deputy."

Clay saw he was getting nowhere with the man. Clay kept his smile on his wind- and sun-burned face. "Wal, I aim to get those men for a hangnoose party some day, Mister Starn, so maybe you ought to cast around for a new manager! That Fogel hellion might not last long."

And then Malcolm Starn said something strange and Clay stared at him.

"Why don't you take a good look at Dave Lansing and his activities? He's — " Starn checked his comments and lowered his head as he sat his saddle, thoughtful.

"Yeah?" Clay questioned, but the other man compressed his lips and rode grimly on in silence. Then Clay continued: "Yes, Dave Lansing is a mighty smooth feller. Hoot and me are watching him. Anything you know about him; anything confidential?"

"Not a thing," he snapped and at that he fed steel to his horse and hit the trail more firmly towards Waco. Clay followed, his big bay taking the journey easily. They came into town as the sun sank on the horizon and the distant hills were already blueish in the evening light. Clay rode up to the sheriff's office and stabled his horse, taking off the saddle and handing over to a hostler. He walked into the office, boots clomping on the boards, and found Hoot at the back of the building locking a drunk Mexican in a cell. Hoot came to Clay as the crazy man yelled abuse. They went into the office and shut the door on the row.

"Now what you got there?" Hoot eyed the pearl-inlaid guns.

They lay on the desk on top of bills of wanted men and other posters. "Bert Fogel's hoglegs," said Clay briefly.

Hoot Sampson's red eyebrows jerked up. "Gawd a'mighty! You are one determined young cuss! You get what you go after."

Clay related his story about encountering Malcolm Starn. The sheriff's eyes were hard and puzzled at the end of this briefing.

For Clay there was an hour's work

examining the guns along with the slug taken from the dead miner's body. He had no equipment beyond a strong magnifying glass and he was following new theories he'd read about. After the initial inspection he knew the slug had been fired from the .44 gun which Fogel would wear in the right-hand holster. The side of this gun was smooth where the weight of the gun lay against the owner's thigh. It was undoubtedly a right-hand gun. And it had fired the slug that had killed the miner.

To prove his point, Clay fired a shot into a sack of corn in the stable. He got the slug and compared it with the one that had killed the man. Both slugs had identical scratches, which showed strongly under the magnifying glass, caused by the barrel. No other .44 gun would mark a bullet in exactly the same way. And there were few .44 guns in Waco, he knew.

Clay spent some time making diagrams and then he was done. He put the evidence before Hoot Sampson and the tough grizzled sheriff knitted his eyebrows as he studied the work.

"You got something, Clay, but I can't say I understand this kind of evidence. I like to catch a galoot red-handed with plenty of witnesses. We can't arrange a hangnoose party on this — what d'you call it? Circumstantial evidence, huh? And we got to put a man afore a judge, an' hanging judges like hard facts."

"We won't act yet," agreed Clay. "We can wait. This kind of evidence will keep."

Hoot nodded. "That Fogel hombre will hang himself and his pals if we give 'em enough rope."

Clay had to put the drawings, the slugs and the guns into a safe. Briefly, he wondered how talk of hangnoose parties and Mary Lester would mix. It would be a dreadful day when he had to give evidence before a judge that would hang Rolf Lester. How could he ever face her again?

It was time for chow because he was starving. He and Hoot went along to the Chinese eating house. They left the wild Mexican prisoner in the cell singing crazy songs in Spanish.

They enjoyed a good meal. There was one point about the Chink's chow; there was plenty of it for a hungry man. They each had a hunk of hot pie, lavishly surrounded by beans. Mugs of coffee steamed beside the plate. They finished with molasses and milk bread. Hoot Sampson wiped his mouth on his gaberdine shirt sleeve.

"Not bad for a Chink. You figure a man ought to marry a Chink, Deputy? Seems the only way a galoot can get regular chow!"

"Better if a guy married a woman," returned Clay.

Hoot shot him a look from under his bushy eyebrows. "Yeah — now I heard Mary Lester can cook real fine. Are you ever going to do somethin' about that?"

"This ain't the best of times."

They walked slowly through the darkness to the office. As they opened a door with a key big enough to shoe a horse, a man sidled towards them. He had been waiting in the darkness of the gable end.

"Sheriff, I gotta talk to you."

Hoot and Clay turned. Clay knew the man as Tom Week, a wrangler who sometimes worked at the Circle Four when the ranch was extra busy. The man sometimes stayed nights at the ranch but other times he slept as a lodger in Waco. The man was plainly uneasy.

"Shoot," said the sheriff. "What you chokin' for?"

"Not here. I don't want to be seen. Let's git inside — I been waitin' a long time for you."

"We've been getting chow. We badge-toters do have to eat."

The taciturn oldster slipped into the office as soon as the door opened and the other two followed. Before Hoot could get the lamp burning properly,

Tom Week began to deliver his news with uncharacteristic speed.

"You know I ain't no gun-toter, Sheriff. I minds me own business, just go on working at the Circle Four when they give me the work — which ain't so often."

"Wal, so what, man?"

"I've been seeing things which I maybe ought not. Ain't none o' my business — except I like Miss Lester an' ain't so keen on her danged brothers: except one's dead now." And the man glanced at Clay. "Wal, I got it figured to tell you."

"What's biting you, old-timer?" Hoot turned to the man.

"You'd better get along to Crag's End with a posse. There's a locomotive going through just before sunup, which gives you plenty of time."

"I know about that loco. It's regular."

"There's a gang aiming to derail it at Crag's End."

"Spill it. How come you know this?"

"A lot of unknown men met up at

the Circle Four ranch-house. Maybe they thought I was invisible — or didn't matter. I tend to be treated that away; and anyway I wasn't supposed to be in the house, just attending a sick cayuse. But I heard. I heard Rolf tellin' that lazy skunk, Seth Mundy, just what they figured to do: derail the locomotive at Crag's End."

"What is the railroad carrying this time that's so valuable?"

"I dunno, Sheriff. I didn't hear much, but I know what I heard. I just skedaddled and got my hoss. There was plenty of them gun-totin' breeds from Pueblo and a new feller with Rolf an' Seth."

"Fogel," commented Clay.

He was already reaching for a Winchester from the rack in the office. Rapidly, he filled his belt with steel-jacketed shells. He had plenty of Colt ammunition.

"Must be more gold, or a payroll," supplied Hoot.

"Just before sunup. We got all night

even allowing for the ride."

"Must be bankers' money. Payroll stuff. Now, look, Clay, we got to get some rest. You can't sleep on a horse."

"Some men say you can."

"We've had a hard time lately. We rest, I say."

"Yeah. There's a lot of beef in the town's corrals. Maybe that money is arriving to pay for that beef."

"How is Mary Lester?" Clay asked of Tom Week. "Does she know what is going on at the ranch?"

"Wal, I dunno. Anyway, Rolf locked her in her room, I knowed that much."

Clay's eyes clouded with anger. A sudden idea hit his mind — but it would have to wait.

Hoot Sampson went over to the Cattleman's Association office and, late as it was, found two men there. As ranchers with a stake in the town, they responded immediately. "Sure, we'll ride as deputies in your posse. It's our duty."

Get some rest. We'll head out in good time afore sunup.

Hoot was wise enough not to go near the Bonanza Saloon for further men; he'd get the men he wanted in time. He did not want the news spread around that a posse was being organised, that might tip off men sympathetic to the bandits and the leader might still be in town. But he got in touch with the kind of man he wanted by stealth. He swore them in and told them to be ready to ride out; and that was a good hour before sunup. A fast ride would take them to Crag's End and in the meantime they could rest.

The plan went ahead. The posse rode out of town two at a time and without any noise. Waco was in silence when they rode.

Once out of town the leaders cantered their horses and soon they formed a bunch. A few miles out on the trail and the night air lightened considerably. Eight grim men bunched together and hoofs cut the ground. The

158

horses pounded across grass land, now yellow with the summer heat and lack of rain. They trusted to the animals to keep a sure footing. There were jackrabbit holes, chunks of rock and shale to test the horses, but the light was improving as dawn was indicated.

To Clay, as he threw questions and got replies from the other men, the setup became clear. The incoming train carried a safe full of currency in bills. Some of the money was for the banks, to meet withdrawals, and some for the well-paid workers in the gold mine. Apparently this news had just got around. Clay and the sheriff had been out of town so much, riding the trails, that they were out of touch.

He knew about Crag's End of course. The railroad line wound through some rocky country six or eight miles off the imaginary Texas-Mexico border, a place of disputes over boundary lines at any time. The track went through numerous rock-bound defiles where a train could easily be halted or derailed.

Rolf Lester had slipped up in overlooking the self-effacing Tom Week.

One of the possemen knew the train's schedule well. And there was little time to waste if they wanted to get there in time to stop a derailment.

Away to the west the river wandered over its rocky bed and so the nearby terrain was not all desert. The horses did skirt occasional clumps of greasewood and chaparral. Dust began to coat the band of riders as, grim and silent, they pressed the horses into full lope. Soon the sky became light and real sunup would arrive with a rush.

Now in the rocky country, they had to slow the pace and allow the animals to find a way in safety. There were red crumbling bluffs on all sides. They rode on until they encountered the double track of line indicating they were near Crag's End. Their nimble horses put down feet on loose rock and shale with accuracy.

They entered the first defile where the lines went through rocky bluffs on both sides. Hoot and Clay were in the lead and as they urged the animals around a bend they saw moving figures a few hundred yards away. The lawmen pulled the horses up and jigged them close to the overhanging bluffs. The rest of the posse crowded in behind them.

We want one man to ride ahead, around that rocky pileup, and try to stop the train afore she gets this far," shouted Clay.

Hoot nodded. "That's right. Who's it gonna be?"

One of the men volunteered and at a nod from Hoot he wheeled his horse and rode away to the left of the lines. He would find a trail without cutting into the holdup men. As the man cantered away, Hoot nodded. "All right, let's work around them galoots. Seems like they're piling rock on the lines. Get all around them and let 'em have some hot lead."

The willing possemen urged mounts further down the defile and then some rode the horses up into steep ledges and paths fit only, it seemed, for deer or goats. They were attempting to spread out.

Clay found himself with two possemen. They rode up a difficult cleft in the side of the defile and then dismounted, hitched the creatures to some tough cactus plants which had roots deep into the yellow, shale-like soil. Even if action started that might spook the animals they would not get away.

Then Clay and the men moved forward, rifles in hand, grim figures who knew the risks they might encounter. They scrambled quickly to positions above the men working at barring the railroad line.

Then, all at once, a rifle shot snapped through the morning air.

"Some feller ran into the holdup rogues!" surmised Clay.

The possemen flung themselves forward, pushing rifles over the edge of the bluff and selecting targets.

The holdup gang on the track were still standing in uncertainty, wondering about the solitary shot, the work of blocking the line halted, when hell burst loose. Clay's rifle roared with the others and two black-garbed men on the line staggered and crashed to the ground.

Rifles spat from the other side of the defile as some men tried to run for cover. Two more spun round as the impact of a bullet hit them. One was in a death dive and the other writhed and screamed in pain.

From the boulders that lined the railroad cut, answering fire proved that a number of holdup men had been hiding while the others put rocks on the line. The sudden shrill whinny of spooked horses proved that the robbers had mounts hidden.

Clay used his Winchester on the bursts of gunfire that flashed from the boulders near the line. Much of the shooting was erratic on both sides, men in sudden fear just blasting off.

Clay waited for more gun-flashes but saw none. As he peered down into the defile, he wondered if the holdup men had all stopped a bullet. He did not think so. But there was a sudden silence, an end to the crack of guns. Once a rifle spoke from high up on the other side of the railroad cut, but that was a solitary shot.

All at once he heard the sudden clatter of horses' hoofs further down the defile, indicating an attempt at getaway on the part of the ambushed holdup men. At the rapid clatter of hoofs, rifles snapped out instantly. Down the rocky-bound defile a bunch of riders were making a mad attempt at escape, spurring the animals mercilessly. The riders were low in the saddles but as the guns cracked the air two men fell as the animals were hit. The fallen horses kicked in terror. The other riders were madly jerking figures in the morning light, disappearing around a bend in the defile. Shots were flung at them, erratically in the circumstances. The men had had the luck of their breed for not one man toppled.

The possemen scrambled down to the flat bed of the railroad cut. They ran for their horses, collecting reins. Clay was one of the first to urge his animal down the line. With his rifle rammed into the saddle boot, he crouched low on the cayuse's neck.

In seconds he encountered the two writhing horses that had belonged to the holdup gang. The critturs lay across the line. Clay reined in with the idea of using a bullet or two to end their torment.

He never got his hand near his gun.

A man lurched almost insanely from the rocky hiding-place in the side of the defile. Clay saw the flash of the man's gun. Even as it blinded him, he jabbed cruel spurs into his mount. The animal sprang and reared in fright. Hoofs pawed at the morning light. The jerking movement saved Clay's life. A bullet whistled past his Stetson. It had been planned to smash him between the eyes and death would have been nasty but quick.

With superb horsemanship, Clay hung on while his right hand scooped at his Colt. He spat the bullet at the lurching holdup man even as the fellow levelled his shooting-iron for another shot. Clay's bullet dug into the man and he dropped his gun instantly. He clawed at his guts, yelling in pain, no longer a hero to himself but a guy dying on his feet.

Clay saw that the man was Seth Mundy. He had been lurching unsteadily because he had been previously wounded in the battle.

The unsavoury character lurched on even in death, momentum taking him across the railroad line and then he sprawled. He died in misery, great rasping sounds coming from him. A fitting end to a man who had caused much misery.

The other possemen were crowding behind Clay now. Only one of them had stopped a slug, a flesh wound fortunately. Clay pushed his hardware back into leather.

"Put them hosses out of pain, some feller," he shouted. Then he rowelled his horse and it sprang into a full lope and continued down the line after the escaping remnants of the holdup gang.

There was a clatter of hoofs in a steady drumming sound as the posse rode down the railroad track. The defile turned twice like a snake. It was this twisting that had aided the escape of the bandits. They had got out of sight pretty fast now that the game was over. The posse thundered along the flat bed of the railroad defile for almost a mile without any sign of the bandits. Then the terrain on both sides of the track levelled off into flat shale and brush country. The posse spread out and made an attempt to search but the owl-hoots had gone. They had scattered into the broken country, flogging their animals desperately.

The posse rode on until they reached the halted train. The rancher who had ridden ahead originally had succeeded in stopping the train and steam hissed from the locomotive as the engineers looked down at the possemen. There were armed guards in the car carrying the money. A few passengers had stuck their heads out of windows, apprehensive people who wanted to know what was going on.

"You can take her in now," yelled the sheriff to the engineer. "The line is clear. We got rid of them holdup agents; but take it easy. How fast does this outfit travel?"

"Reckon we can get up to twenty-five miles an hour," bawled the man.

Hoot rubbed dust out of his red moustache and stared at the hissing steel monster. "Gawd — that's too fast for a man to travel. How do you breathe?"

Some minutes later, with a mournful wail, the locomotive began to heave the load forward and the passengers shut the windows and no doubt confabbed about the troubles on the railroad.

The posse rode back through the defile, behind the train. Clay and the sheriff stopped to examine the dead men who had been laid to one side. Neither Rolf Lester nor Bert Fogel were among the bodies. Hoot claimed to recognise one or two ruffians who had given trouble in Waco and the area in the past but he wasn't too sure.

"Dead is sure dead," he said in satisfaction.

The others were unknown renegades probably from distant parts. Their adventures were over — along with their greed.

Clay stopped to go through Seth Mundy's pockets in the hope that the man might carry some document or provide some clue as to the real organiser of the holdup, but there was nothing. He had not been very hopeful. Men like Seth Mundy could hardly read, anyway.

"That's the end of his trail," grunted

the sheriff. "Aw, let's get back to town. Maybe we've got some other hellions in Waco kicking up a shindig by now!"

But Clay had other ideas. Trail-tired although he was, he spoke out. "I'm going across to the Circle Four. I just don't like leaving Mary Lester out there with those trouble-makers. Maybe I can't do much but I sure want to go over there."

"You ought to get that gal up before a preacher," grunted Hoot.

Clay looked rueful. "I got my loop tangled right now. I killed one brother and now I'm working on Rolf for a hangnoose. I figure the odds are stacked against me and Mary ever hitting it off."

He left the sheriff with the other riders and turned his animal towards the distant Circle Four ranch. Time went by swiftly as man and horse covered the relatively flat terrain. Feeling fatigue due to much time in the saddle, he hunched low and conserved his energy. The miles went under the hoofs of the strong animal as the morning sun rose higher to heat the land. He went on doggedly, one thought only: he just had to see Mary. But how could he explain?

Then the ranch buildings loomed up, cattle in small herds searching for green grass, and then he encountered the cottonwoods, motionless because there was not a movement of air. The silence of the land was broken only by the mournful sound of cattle.

Eventually Clay rode slowly into the ranch-yard, dismounted and threw the reins over some corral poles. He stood still for some minutes while he rolled a cigarette and lit it, thinking, wondering what he would say to the girl. There wasn't a sign of movement around the place, except for the distant cattle. He wondered if Rolf Lester had returned from the fracas at the railroad line. He figured he would find out pretty quick.

Taking a last draw on the brown-paper cigarette, he dropped it to the dusty yard and ground it with the heel of his boot. He walked slowly towards the porch steps, thinking with a troubled mind. Suddenly he thought that gunplay and hard riding were easier than this doubt. He was not quite sure what he wanted to say or do. He was just like any other young man who is worried about a girl who means a lot to him. He just wanted to see Mary and reassure her that he was present to help, if needed.

He rapped on the door firmly, He heard footsteps. They sounded like a man's high-heel riding boots. Waiting, he knew Mary was not coming to the door, not surprising in a lawless country late at night. The door opened and Clay found himself staring into a pointed gun. Behind the gun was a male face.

Dave Lansing's saturnine face!

"Why, hello, Deputy!" The man smiled and lowered his gun. "This ain't my house but I guess I can ask you to come right in."

The owner of the Bonanza Saloon put his gun down by his side. He was wearing his black suit, white shirt and black necktie. His trousers were tucked into riding boots but he had no holster.

"What are you doing here?" Clay strode cautiously into the house.

"Just visiting," murmured Lansing.

They entered the big living-room with its Indian rugs and large stone fireplace. The night was cooling after the heat of the day, usual in this area of Texas, and a fire had been lit.

Clay came face to face with Mary Lester and Rolf. Dave Lansing put the gun down on the top of a black oak dresser as if he had merely picked the gun up for the purpose of coming to the door — or been handed it! Clay searched the girl's face and saw at once the trace of past tears.

"Hello, Mary. Are you all right?"

"Sure, she's all right," rasped Rolf Lester. "Why the heck shouldn't she be?"

173

Clay turned a grim face to him. "I figured she might be worried and upset."

"She ain't. What's she got to worry about? An' what the hell is it to you, badge-toter?"

"You've been out with the gang that was all set to rob the train."

"What's all this about a train?" Dave Lansing asked quickly.

"Don't you know? A holdup gang tried to derail the cars. There was currency on board. But it didn't come off. Some hell-bents got shot instead."

Mary's eyes were wide with fear. Clay continued grimly. "Where's Seth Mundy?"

"In town, I reckon," snapped Rolf.

Clay hit the other man with harsh words. "You're lying. Seth Mundy is dead, an' you know it. I put the slug in his hide myself. He was killed as part of the gang trying to hold up the train."

Mary's hand went to her mouth and she shook her head helplessly as if words terrified her.

"You know Seth ain't in town," continued Clay, looking at Rolf Lester. "And you were with him and the rest of the robbing outfit."

The other's blue eyes were bright with fury. "If you must know every durned thing, lawman, I ain't been out of this ranch-house."

Clay refused to bandy words. He merely stared at the other man's hate-filled blue eyes and knew he was lying all the way.

Rolf Lester's lips twisted in a travesty of a smile. He turned to Dave Lansing. "Ain't that right, Dave?"

"Sure is. We ain't been anywhere. Just moseying around this ranch."

Rolf Lester snarled at his sister. "Ain't that right, Mary?"

She nodded. But Clay noticed she couldn't speak because she was choking with emotion. Clay watched her, full of a desire to take her in his arms and give her reassurance. She stood motionless, as if lying had hurt her like a blow.

Clay took out the makings and rolled another cigarette. He worked leisurely, waited and watched. The silence was deep in the ranch house, with only the steady ticking of a big clock to mark the passage of time. And then the girl seemed to sob and she turned away and sank to a large rocking-chair.

"You know darned well you were in that holdup gang," said Clay evenly. He flicked a glance at Dave Lansing who stood near the oak dresser. "That's the second time you've alibied Rolf. What do you get out of all this, Lansing?"

The man smiled suavely. "Don't you believe me — and Mary? Do you figure us for liars; including Mary?"

"I figure you for a bit of a trickster, Lansing, an' that's saying it to your face. You'll be tellin' me that Seth Mundy was here all day."

Lansing shrugged and retained his imperturbable smile. Rolf Lester glared with unrelenting animosity and looked as if he'd sooner use a gun than talk any further. Mary sat in the chair with downcast eyes.

Clay expelled smoke. "Mary — I should have asked your permission to smoke. Do you mind?"

"She does!" snarled Rolf. "You can git, lawman! Get outa here!"

Clay continued, "I hope you know what you're doing, Lester, bringing all this trouble on your sister."

"We ain't in trouble!"

Clay eyed him narrowly. There was something strange about the way he sat in his chair behind the table. It was not like the bull-headed Rolf Lester to sit still while the man he hated intruded in his own home.

"You ain't in trouble, huh?" Clay moved swiftly, unexpectedly.

He strode around the table and gripped him by the shoulder, pulling the big young buckeroo around in his seat, the man making an attempt to resist but too late.

Clay saw the blood-soaked bandage wrapped around his arm. He had been hiding the wound behind the table.

"So you got plugged?"

"You're one smart hombre! But you jump fences too fast. I shot myself just an hour ago — an accident — got careless with a blamed Colt while cleaning it."

Clay went to the door, hard-faced. "I can't talk to liars. Sorry, Mary. Maybe we can meet and talk some time without interruption."

"You can leave her alone! Git! You'll meet me — on the end of a smokepole!"

Clay turned at the last moment. "You and Lansing are two mighty smart hombres. But watch it. I've got a hunch you're both bent for boothill!"

7

CLAY MANDELL rode his bay back to Waco as the kerosene lamps made patches of light in the main street. He was tired of riding and grimly sick of events that were parting him from Mary Lester. He got to the stable at the back of the office and put the horse to feed and rest.

He found that the sheriff was out somewhere so he went to his room and washed the trail dust from his body. He felt better after putting on a clean shirt and buckling on his holster belt again, checking the gun.

He went out into the main stem and proceeded to the Last Chance. Full of men, with some ladies of doubtful reputation, there was plenty of money going over the counter.

He figured he could do with a shot of whisky. He set his eyes on Bert Fogel who was standing behind the counter with an amused look. The man was dressed in brown trousers and a clean black shirt which rippled tight across his chest.

Clay caught his eye. "Whisky, Mister Fogel, please, and make it your best."

"We only sell the best. An' I ain't the bartender." But he came over with a bottle and a glass.

"You been attending to business all night?" Clay asked.

"Yeah, more or less."

"Maybe I can ask the customers if you've been here all night," murmured Clay.

Fogel's eyes glinted. "You do that. But remember I got an office at the back. I've been in there a lot."

"Bit of a change from gun-toting."

Dark eyes glinted back at Clay.

"How come Starn picked on you for this job?" Clay asked bluntly.

"Ain't that my business?" Fogel grated back.

Clay left the saloon, wandered the

length of Waco's town limits and turned a block and found what he was looking for. There was a legend above a false-fronted building: MALCOLM STARN FREIGHT COMPANY. It was impressive if a bit shabby. Clay knew Starn had a home at the back of the premises, which was usual in frontier towns, because although the name 'Texas' derives from the word 'Tejas', meaning friend, Waco could be anything but friendly.

Clay knocked on the door three times before he realised he wasn't getting an answer. On a hunch he walked around to the back and stood in an alley, figuring to speak to Starn about Bert Fogel. Maybe he could twist some clue out of the freight-line owner.

Suddenly a light behind a blind-covered window went dark. It seemed someone had realised there was a watcher. Clay walked across the road and stood in the dark shadows of a building and waited. He had to be patient. Then he was about to turn away when he heard the creak of a door being opened. He stayed hidden and alert for a few more seconds then he saw a back shadow of a guy leaving Starn's place. Clay crossed over with grim strides and was beside the man before the unknown realised the fact.

Clay put out a hand and gripped the man by the wrist. In the darkness he still wasn't sure who he'd encountered. Clay heard an exclamation of pain and then he saw the man's face reasonably clearly. The guy was Malcolm Starn. Then Clay withdrew his hand and looked at the stickiness on it. Blood!

"How did it happen?" snapped the deputy.

He got the evasive answer he expected. "I had an accident, Mandell. Shot my wrist with a damned Colt."

"Thought you never used a gun?"

"No more I do. But I got to looking at the gun I keep in the office and the damned thing exploded."

"I'll take you along to Doc Hawton."

They roused the doctor from a game of poker with one of his old pals, and Starn got his wound attended while he repeated his story. Clay did not believe a word of the halting tale. This was the second account of a hombre who just had an accident with a gun!

On the way back to the sheriff's office, alone, Clay pondered over the events. Had Starn some stake in the robberies that had happened? Had he been wounded in the rataplan of shooting down by the railroad? There was no need to wonder where Rolf Lester had got his wound, but how about Starn?

Clay went to bed that night and slept soundly. Conjecture was all very interesting but in the rough climate of Waco's life only seeing and believing had any importance.

The next morning, as they went for eats, he told Hoot Sampson how he had found Rolf Lester at the Circle Four with Dave Lansing. The Chinaman welcomed them as regular customers and set out eggs and bacon.

"Dave Lansing plays a tricky hand," growled Hoot. "How come that man is so ready to alibi the Lester buckeroo? And Mary Lester tellin' lies to save her no-good brother! Hell!"

"Well, maybe we'll understand some day why Starn hires Fogel," added Clay. "And maybe we'll discover how he got that wound."

"The hell with them all!" growled Hoot. "Enjoy your breakfast, young feller."

They were in the stable some time later, tightening the cinches on their horses, when someone darkened the patch of light at the door.

Clay wheeled fast. "Mary!"

He was beside her swiftly, searching his eyes. "Why are you here?"

"I wanted to see you," she faltered. For a moment she seemed reluctant to speak. Then: "Rolf and a man called Bert Fogel are riding south today. I want you to stop them, Clay."

"What are they doing ridin' south?"

"I overheard." She seemed to choke. "They're going to meet the boss and break into a placer mining camp lower down on the Rio Pecos."

"Gold again," muttered Clay and she nodded and replied. "Yes. This camp is more than forty miles away, a place called Monument Valley."

He nodded. "I know. But how do I handle Rolf? With a gun?"

"Stop him from ever reaching the camp." She laid a hand on his arm, her eyes appealing, so much he wanted to sweep her into his arms.

"How come Rolf can ride? Ain't his arm botherin' him?"

"He's so hard."

"Was Fogel at the Circle Four this morning?"

"Yes. He came over very early."

"They don't let the grass grow under their feet," he muttered. "Have these trouble-bent men set off, Mary?"

"They'll be on their way by now, obviously. You'll be able to catch up with some fast riding."

185

Hoot Sampson gloated. "We can catch the varmints red-handed. I'll arrange a posse. Just what we want. Hangnoose for the lot of 'em — or lead poisoning!"

"Wait!" Mary Lester stopped the sheriff. "I don't want a posse after Rolf. I just asked you to stop him ever getting to Monument Valley. You've just got to stop him, Clay. Please! I don't want him caught in the act of robbing!"

Clay moistened dry lips. "Mary," he began.

"Will you just stop Rolf from reaching the camp? I don't care what happens to Fogel. I just want Rolf stopped. He's — he's my brother, Clay!"

Clay swung to Hoot Sampson. "You're the sheriff. What's it to be?"

"We're a-goin' to catch any skunk red-handed shootin' into that camp. Maybe they'll stop lead — or maybe they'll end up as candidates for a hanging judge."

With surprising speed Mary drew a small Derringer from within her skirt pocket and pointed the gun determinedly at them. The sheriff froze, anger glinting in his eyes. "Put away that gun, gal!"

"Don't move — either of you!" Mary's voice was hard.

Clay was almost shocked into silence.

You're not going to catch Rolf red-handed at anything!" she said determinedly. "You'll either do as I want, or you'll stay here for as long as I can hold you. That'll give Rolf plenty of time to get away. There won't be a posse after him."

Clay looked at the sheriff. "What do we do?"

For a moment Hoot Sampson glared, and then he relented. "All right. Let's hit leather. Anyhow, I figure a lawman's job is to stop robbery as much as catch the villains who did it!"

Mary replaced the Derringer in her pocket with a sigh of relief. "I'm going with you."

Clay held her arm. "No, Mary. Monument Valley is desert type country, all hard going an' too much for a woman. And there'll be trouble."

"I'm a-going, Clay!"

In the next few minutes Hoot led the horses out and filled water bottles while the deputy tried to argue with her. But she would not change her mind. "I'm going, Clay. I want to be there. And what makes you think a woman can't do as well as a man?"

Like many a guy before him he gave up. She had a wiry pony outside and had prepared for the ride. A canteen of water was tied to the saddle horn and a rifle was in the saddle holster.

They rode out as the sun climbed the sky and promised heat. Hoot Sampson was grimly disgruntled but he kept his word and did not call for a posse. He knew anything could happen. Mary Lester was a naive young filly to think Rolf would be easily handled without gunplay.

As they cantered south along the

banks of the river Rio Pecos, where grass grew green in spite of the scorching sun, and in former years the bison had roamed, they spotted occasional herds of beef.

Clay tried to get some information from Mary. "Have you any idea who this boss hombre might be?"

"All Rolf and Fogel said was something about meeting up with the boss man. I didn't really hear very much — and I was scared in case they saw me. I did get the facts about Monument Valley. Rolf told Fogel how much some placer miners were pulling out of the river. On the impulse I rode out."

Clay nodded. He stared through the heat haze. "Monument Valley. The camp is nothing but a lot of tents and shacks made out of tin cans and driftwood hauled out of the river. Yes, those miners are panning gold all right but it's a hard life and if they can win gold good luck to 'em. That don't mean they got to be robbed."

"Why does Rolf have to live like a hellion?"

"He's just wild. He's bull-strong and reckless."

"And Fogel's a gunny. How about your ranch? Isn't it a good enough living?"

"Scrub is growing on the land all the time. We got title to miles of land but every year the desert claims more of it. We're not in the best area for cattle rearing, as you know. Rolf and I own a half-share in the deeds. That was part of my Dad's will. So maybe Rolf thinks he can make more by robbing and stealing. Oh, God, what can I do?"

"We shall see," Clay muttered.

Hoot Sampson was impatient because they were not making enough haste, so Clay rowelled his horse and he and Mary went at full lope following the twisting river course. The Rio Pecos was entering rocky channels now. Away in the distance, many miles, towering buttes with red, scoured walls rose from the plain. Here at certain seasons harsh winds, full of sand and rain, smoothed the buttes like sandpaper on wood. As they rode they searched the horizon for sign of other riders. But in the heat hazes they often fancied they could see objects.

And then like slowly moving dots they caught sight of moving animals, horses and riders. The distant riders moved slowly along the red face of a vast cliff, the speed walking pace. As Clay squinted through the glare of the sun, the distant objects seemed to progress like snails. Hoot Sampson's experienced old eyes had picked them out. "Two of em. Now who are they?"

"Fogel and Rolf?" hazarded Clay.

"We can stop them!" cried Mary. "Hurry!"

"Those fellers are dangerous," snapped Hoot. "And they can do us a good turn."

"What do you mean?" asked the girl.

"I mean I aim to let those jiggers

catch up with this big boss feller. I'd like to identify that galoot."

"You're trying to trick me!"

"I ain't," snapped the sheriff. "But I'm anxious to set eyes on this boss feller. I promise you, gal, that these men won't start raidin' the gold camp. A rifle will do that — but only after I clamp eyes on that boss rannigan."

There was nothing Mary could do. It was futile to argue with the hard old sheriff. Clay left the situation at that.

Hoot took charge and led the way, riding across the plain to the left. They traversed hot hard-baked sand, with the cover of a red butte between them and the distant riders. Hoot cut a trail that led ahead of the two renegade riders so that owing to the position of the line of buttes they could not be observed.

The river had curved, but anyone who wanted to hit Monument Valley with as little riding as possible would not follow the twists of the erratic river. The two men ahead were riding for some broken country. For a long time the two riders were lost to view, but Hoot was confident of the direction of their trail. Soon great heaps of volcanic boulders lay piled in all directions, like gigantic marbles.

Clay and the other two came round this broken rocky pileup miles from the spot where the sheriff estimated Rolf and Fogel would eventually hit. Then Hoot waved his hand. "I'm goin' to climb to a high spot and take a look-see for those galoots. They can't be far from here." And the rugged sheriff went up the sloping face of a huge slab of rock. Clay grinned at Mary but the girl responded only with a faint smile.

A bit later Hoot slid down from his high perch, boots scraping on rock. "I think they've met up with the boss. They're having a parley just way off from this pileup and there's three hombres now and they got a spare hoss, too."

They rode out of the cleft in single file. They skirted the pileup until they

193

came to the outcrop that was the last bit of cover between them and the renegade riders. Then Hoot halted his party again.

"Clay, I want you to go over the top of this heap and get around to the other side of them fellers. I'll give you plenty of time but make it quick. Then when you see me ride out with a rifle fixed on 'em, you walk out of cover from the other side. We trap 'em like that!"

Clay nodded. He dismounted and threw his reins to Mary and got his rifle from the saddle holster. He went up the rocky pileup, taking care not to go near the edge that sloped into the desert. He made little noise but swift progress. He judged a spot to make for. He encountered the spined cholla cactus and prickly pear and thought that maybe a rattler or two might be basking in these rocks.

Eventually he found his spot. He could see the position that concealed Hoot Sampson and there was nothing more to do but wait on events. So he gripped his rifle and watched. Out on the red desert, less than five hundred yards away, the three riders were squatting on the sand. They were smoking while the horses stood with hanging heads, suffering from the heat in this arid part of the land.

Clay fancied he could identify Rolf Lester even though he could see only his back. Bert Fogel in his black outfit was easily spotted. Clay wasn't sure of the third man; there was nothing about his build or his clothes that he could recognise. "Got it all planned. I wonder who is that third jigger?"

Then, with silent drama, a horse nosed out of the distant outcrop. The man was Hoot Sampson, with his rifle levelled high over the animal's head. And behind came Mary, leading Clay's bay horse.

Clay walked out at the same moment, rifle ready, tensed as was natural. He heard Hoot bawl: "Hoist 'em!"

"Don't reach!" shouted Clay from the other side.

The three men promptly stuck their hands above their shoulders. Rolf was the first to get slowly to his feet, his hands high. He turned to see Winchesters pointing at him from two sides.

Hoot rode closer and stopped ten yards from the group. Clay came up from the opposite direction and halted. Fogel turned slowly and flicked sardonic glances first at Hoot and then at Clay. The third man turned and scowled. Clay stared at the man. He was a nondescript ruffian with the appearance of an owl-hoot written all over his unshaven visage. Clay had never seen him in his life, but he knew instinctively that this man was not the unknown person known as the boss. The man was just another hired gunny it seemed!

Hoot Sampson's thoughts were on the same level as Clay's and there was sheer disgust written on his face. Even his red moustache bristled. "Who are you, feller?" he bawled.

The man scowled again. "What the hell's it to you, lawman?"

"Just a little joke from Sheriff Sampson," drawled Fogel. "He's got such a suspicious mind he can't abide seeing three waddies ride out together."

Rolf sneered, enjoying the sheriff's setback. The sheriff went on, bawling in anger, "Listen, scum, I know you figure to ride into the gold miners' camp and grab dust and nuggets — that's what you're out here for instead of taking your ease in Waco."

"Is that so! You're all tangled, Sheriff," jeered Rolf. "We don't know what the hell you're talkin' about!"

Rolf's gaze fixed on his sister, and the cold inhuman gleam scared the girl. Clay did not miss a thing.

"This ain't no pow-pow," snapped Hoot. "I did figure to see this mysterious boss man but I didn't ride out this way just to cross words with scum."

"You can cut out that talk," hissed

Bert Fogel. "No guy talks like that to me."

"You lot can ride back to Waco, right now. With me keeping this rifle on your backs. And Clay here is goin' to ride into Monument Valley and warn the miners about you skunks in case you try to put your plans into operation another day."

Hoot had hardly got his angry words out when a rifle spoke with sudden menace. The gun flashed and spat. He lurched in the saddle, dropping his rifle and clutching at his side, with blood spurting through his fingers in a horrifying rush. As his horse jibbed in fear at the gun shot, he fell from his saddle and hit the ground with a terrible thud. In seconds the scene had changed. That was the way of guns.

Clay had wheeled with the blast of the rifle in his ears. He saw a man advance from a pile of boulders, carrying a smoking rifle, and there was a bandana masking most of his face.

Clay whipped his own rifle up but he

was too slow for the other man had the advantage of split-second surprise. The other man's gun flashed its message of threatening death once more. Clay was caught out, desperately levelling his own weapon.

Instantly pain seared through Clay's head. A million jagged lights flashed before his eyes. There was time only for one thought — the masked man was surely the mysterious boss!

Then thought died in a mile-deep pit of total darkness. Clay knew he was falling, into a terrible chasm, with blackness of infinity before him.

He pitched forward as if already dead!

8

MARY LESTER was stricken with the horror of it. She watched Clay pitch forward and with terror shuddering through her she could not move a limb. Hoot Sampson, too, lay sprawled on the desert sand, and she could see the red patch on his shirt, something that sickened her. Dazedly, she turned her head to her brother but all she could see was the savage grin on his face. He lumbered forward through the thick sandy soil and stared down at the motionless body of Clay Mandell.

"Guess you fixed this swine good an' proper!" he snarled to the approaching man.

The unknown turned his head and pointed the rifle at Mary. "I should deal with her!"

Rolf Lester's twisted smile faded very

slowly. "She's my sister."

"She could be dangerous to us."

"You're masked, ain't you?" Rolf snapped.

Mary sat in the saddle numb with the horror. Too late she remembered the Derringer she carried in her skirt pocket. If she tried to get it out, the stranger would kill her, she knew.

"I had to get you hombres out of a bad spot," sneered the boss. "And a good thing these damned fools didn't figure you were waiting for me to ride up. Maybe it was lucky for you I was kinda late."

Rolf swung to his sister. "You must have put these men on to our trail."

"That makes her dangerous, as I have said," commented the masked boss. Rolf swung back at him.

Quit worryin' about her. I'll take her in hand. She won't give no trouble, boss. And she can't split on you. She don't know you from Adam.

"All right. Get to your horses, we're ridin' to the gold camp. Those placer miners are loaded with dust an' nuggets, it's been reported to me."

The men grabbed reins and leaped to leather. In that second the shock drained out of Mary and she slid from her saddle and went swiftly to Clay. It came like a revelation to her to realise how much she really cared for this tall, slow-speaking westerner. She reached him and noticed the red blood welling from the side of his head. She was trying to comfort him when Rolf's hand gripped her arm and jerked her to her feet.

"Get on your horse, sister. I didn't shoot him, anyway, the boss did. You'll have to come along with us."

She tried to struggle but he held her and found the Derringer, taking it and shoving the gun into his belt. Then he practically pushed her onto her horse and, helpless, she wanted to cry. She felt she couldn't fight any more. Clay must be dead: and Hoot was either dead or dying.

"All right, let's get going!" snapped the boss.

The four men formed round the girl's animal, forcing the brute on as they fed rowells to sweating flanks. The pack went into a full lope. Rolf, Fogel, the boss man and the typical range ruffian who apparently was known as Clip, all headed out across the desert and scrub terrain.

Two riderless horses were left, nosing for tufts of desert grass. And on the ground two men sprawled.

Mary Lester felt utter dismay at her own helplessness, knowing nothing could turn her brother from the path he was taking. Lawlessness seemed to be in his blood. The riders went swiftly, not in silence but making coarse jokes about the fool miners and the gold they'd pick up. The boss man kept his mask in place.

Monument Valley lived up to the name with fantastic red buttes and rocky pinnacles. Erosion by wind and rain, in the winters, had carved many marvellous contours. The river, now low in water in the summer months, wound erratically. There was one red butte which hugged the river, and the riders came close to the high walls and slowed to a walk. And there, in a flat plain of sand and shale, was the main placer camp. Tents and shacks lined the course of the river. The place was a sorry ramshackle dump. The men who slaved all day in the heat were winning gold from the water; but slowly, some on a bonanza and others barely making a living. The river was running low and soon the gold would cease to run down from the hills: until the winter brought fresh deposits.

The area was a hive of industry. Men were working on small dams, panning the silt and water for the minute chips and flecks of gold. Men sweated with aching backs as they stood in water.

"Nice hard workers!" sneered the masked boss. "All right, don't make a noise. We ride down nice an' slow, spread out, and then at a signal from me we make those panners reach for the sky. They ain't wearing guns while they work. The gold they've got is stacked in them shacks and tents. That's where you come in, Clip. Your job is to get among them tents an' shacks and get the gold that's bagged while we keep the fool miners on the end of guns. Work fast, amigo. You'll get some gold: better than slavin' for it, huh?"

The horses of the four hell-bents were sniffing at the water and getting restless and so it was time to start the action. The horses picked a way slowly along the ridge that led down to the river. The men ignored Mary. Soon the renegades were spaced out, surprise their advantage.

"Hoist 'em!" shouted the boss, his rifle a menace to any miner who figured to get reckless. Rolf and Fogel added similar commands and pointed guns at the mining groups. All along the river, within rifle range, miners straightened backs to realise they were covered by robbers' guns. It was a complete holdup — while Clip was among the shacks and tents, grabbing at gold bags and tossing them into a heap.

The element of surprise was with the robbers. They sat tall, high on their horses. Rolf and Fogel had pulled bandanas up over mouths, as if to match with the boss man. Hats were well down. Only glinting, savagely amused eyes stared over the scene and did not miss a thing. The man named Clip was busy going through the tents and shacks entering with a Colt in hand. Luck was with him because all the miners were down at the river. He grabbed at anything that resembled a gold poke. In one or two places he couldn't find a gold bag and, swearing obscenely, lurched to the next stop.

He pushed at one tent and saw a haggard man lying on the floor. He was apparently ill. The miner raised a gun with two hands that shook. But Clip's shooting-iron roared first and the slug flattened against bone, tearing a hole in the miner's head.

He kicked around the tent but there was no gold to be found. Angrily, he stamped out and plunged into a nearby shack. Clip carried a canvas bag and pretty soon it was fairly full and heavy. Gold was a heavy metal even in small quantities and he went on greedily, into the next tent, and from there to another shack. His bag full and heavy, he threw gold dust pokes into a heap at a nearby spot.

Down at the river the miners were getting restless. One man had a gun stuck in his belt. He was the only armed man and he figured to use his gun on the nearest masked raider. Fingers itching while the other miners cursed and threatened, he moved imperceptibly.

All at once rage consumed the miner and he leaped forward, foolishly, the gun in his fist. It spat lead at the unknown boss but the bullets went wide as the miner shook with rage. He was the poorest of gunmen.

The boss's rifle spoke. It belched

red flame and the aim was swift and accurate. The miner threw up his arms, dropped his handgun and crashed into the river bed shale. He was really dead.

Some minutes later, while the placer miners shook impotent fists and others froze under the pointed rifles, Clip gave his shrill whistle. It was a signal that he had cleaned up so far as possible in the limited time. The three masked riders jigged the horses crab-wise up the sloping river bank and not for a second did the Winchesters cease to menace. Clip worked fast, tying the canvas bag and other pokes to the saddle of the spare horse. He was gloating over the prospect of being rich — even if only for a limited time! Even with the boss taking the bigger share, there was enough to keep a man in drink and females for a long time — and all for a day's work!

The riders withdrew to the limits of the mining camp, rifles still keeping control. "Let's git!" shouted Rolf Lester.

Four riders and a spare horse turned away from the river and got into a cloud of dust raised by horses' hoofs — and only then did Rolf realise that Mary had vanished from the scene. He turned and stared in all directions but he could not see his sister. Then it was all fast riding in the getaway.

Back at the gold camp at the river, cursing miners rushed for horses and guns, but few of their animals were saddled and time was wasted in confusion. Ultimately some of the miners rode out in a straggly line a good way behind the robbers, who were making good speed into the distance. Fifteen minutes later, at flying speed, they were well into the broken terrain, taking advantage of gullies and valleys. The boss had planned well.

Mary Lester had turned her pony even before the raid had started. There was nothing she could do to stop the robbers and, in fact, she was obsessed with only one notion. She just had to return to where Hoot Sampson and

Clay lay. It was awful to think they might be dead, but she had to go back to where the men sprawled so dreadfully in the desert land. How could she help them? She wasn't sure. Maybe they *were* dead!

She went on taking a direct course through the red buttes of Monument Valley, her good sense of direction a big asset in the swift ride. She rode through brush and thorn, galloping her pony out of the red butte country and heading cross the semi-arid plain. In the rocky outcrops there was sustenance for prickly pear and the rattler.

She did not know that four human snakes would make for rocky defiles and shake off the pursuing miners. She headed fast over the plain to the heap of volcanic rock where she knew Clay and Hoot had been shot. As she went swiftly, she wondered about the boss. She had a slight suspicion as to his identity but she was not a hundred per cent sure. She was heartbroken about the way her brother had turned so lawless. She couldn't understand his mentality — and Tad had gone the same way! She flung her grim thoughts from her.

She skirted the large rocky island in the sand and shale, and then, suddenly it seemed, she came upon the two shot men and their horses. She saw Clay sitting up, attending to the sheriff, who was now propped against a rock. Mary leaped from her mount and ran to Clay.

Her soft bronzed face showed her love for this man, even as she noticed the ugly red wound along the side of his head. He'd been creased, sent unconscious by the searing bullet. She flung her arms around him. "Oh, Clay — you're alive, thank God!"

He grinned. "Just about, Mary, alive and groggy."

She looked at Hoot. "Is he okay?"

"He's just alive. Gawd knows if he'll stay that way. The bullet went through him — and out, I think! He's lost a lot of blood. You can see it in the sand."

She had noticed the sickening red pool. She glanced up as something flew with flapping wings across the blue sky.

"Vultures," muttered Clay. "They've been around ever since I swam back into this world. Wal, we've got to reach Waco, somehow, Mary. If we can only git to horseback."

"Yes, Waco and Doc Hawton — and it's a lot of riding. But we can do it. I can help you get Hoot to a saddle, and we'll tie him on somehow."

"No need. I'll ride with him on my bay. Reckon the hoss can take double. Hoot would fall off by himself, but I can hold him steady."

She nodded. "Yes — of course." She watched as Clay used two bandanas to provide a tight bandage around the sheriffs middle to stem the bleeding. Then between them, with some effort, they managed to raise the barely-conscious sheriff to the saddle and Clay mounted, but without his usual lithe swing. He hunkered down on the

212

leather, gripped Hoot, steadied him as he sat heavily in front of him. Then Mary got to her saddle and the other horse followed as they set off. For Clay, everything was a real effort, his head throbbing.

"What has happened, Mary? Fill me in." They rode very slowly, stirrup to stirrup.

"They made me go with them, as you can guess. They raided the placer mining camp and in the confusion I just rode away."

"I wonder if any hellion got killed?"

"I don't know — and I don't care now," she said fiercely, referring to her brother.

"Mary, there ain't nothing I can do for Rolf. He's just hell-bent. You don't hate me for going after him?"

She shook her head. "You've had a job to do, Clay. Oh, when will it all be over?"

He was silent for some moments. Then: "It'll be over when some more men are dead; and when that boss man is brought to justice."

She rode on in silence but he saw the tears, the tremble of her lips. And then she stared proudly ahead and he knew he loved this girl — but as a western man he was a bit inarticulate!

As they progressed slowly across the warm land, three horses, one with a double load, and the girl keeping a lookout, he realised she was fine and lovely. It was incredible that she had a wild brother like Rolf Lester!

As for Clay, his head throbbed and it was difficult to think clearly. He had to keep the sheriff upright in the saddle — or at least prevent him from falling from the horse — and the man's weight was considerable. The shimmering heat was an added problem and the distance back to Waco was going to drain his energy. He was worried about old Hoot. He had lost a lot of blood and the bullet might have caused internal injuries. Only a doctor could diagnose the truth.

Slowly plodding across the land, he

took the chance to ask the girl: "Did you study that boss man?"

She hesitated. Then: "I think he is Dave Lansing."

"Did you see his face?"

"No. I can't be sure. There was just something in his build, the way he sat his horse — something — but I'm not sure."

The ride went on grimly, Clay, gripping his saddle, his head painful, the half-conscious man before him a deadly burden. In the end Clay was barely aware of passing time and the miles, but Mary led the animals on, keeping the plodding pace, her thoughts on the distant Waco and the chance of getting these men to the doc.

Talking was an effort for Clay and so he lapsed into silence, holding his position on the saddle, keeping Hoot from falling, and he was barely aware of time and distance.

They were some miles out of Waco when a cloud of dust denoted riders. She watched, maintaining their plodding pace, tired horses and two wounded men needing her attention. Then the new riders spotted them on the horizon, through the heat haze, and the black shapes of men and animals grew larger. Soon the riders thundered up to Clay and Mary. They saw the deputy badge on Clay's shirt and the newcomers put their guns back into holsters.

"You're miners," said Clay with an expert glance at their mud-spattered pants and vests. "Are you lookin' for those thieving robbers?"

"Yep: what do you know about them, Deputy?" asked a large gaunt Irishman.

"The sheriff and me tried to stop them raidin' your camp. The sheriff got gunned. I've got to get him to the doc in Waco."

The Irishman stared shrewdly, noting the red wound along Clay's head just under his hat. "Sure, and you've been shot yourself." The Irish miner turned to one of his pals. "Joe, you gotta strong cayuse! You can help this deputy man."

Clay was glad of the assistance. Soon Hoot Sampson was transferred to the big black roan which Joe controlled.

"Wal, looks like them skunks have lost us off," growled the gaunt Irish miner. "But if we get 'em we'll string 'em up, Deputy! We rode this-away thinking they were bound for Waco."

"They'll not return to Waco." Clay shook his head —and gave himself another stabbing pain. "And you ought not to take the law into your own hands. We've got a judge in Waco who'll arrange a hangnoose."

"Judge be damned!" roared one miner. "There ain't many trees down by the river but by heck we'll find one if we ever get them robbing swines! Have you any idea who they are, Deputy?"

Clay drew in a deep breath. "Some sort of idea. One feller is called Bert Fogel and he manages the Last Chance Saloon in town."

"Do he now? Guess I'll remember

that name. How about the other hellions?"

"I'm not sure," snapped Clay, and he looked at Mary.

"Wal, we fellers aim to get some satisfaction agin them robbing bastards. A placer feller died. They're murderers, all of 'em."

The miners, with the exception of the man called Joe O'Rourke, turned their horses and went out across the scrub lands again. Joe O'Rourke intended to ride in with the sheriff.

Clay edged his horse close to Mary's pony. Reaching out, he took her hand for a few moments. "You know what this means, my dear? Rolf and Fogel won't dare show up in Waco again. With Hoot an' me alive we could convince a judge that those rannigans raided the gold mining placer camp at the river and killed a man. They won't risk that. They're on the run from now on — owl-hoots with every man's hand against them. We'll get wanted posters out."

She nodded, unhappy. They then edged up with Joe O'Rourke and his burden of the wounded sheriff and continued the ride.

Waco was still some way off. Hoot was seriously wounded. There were tasks to deal with.

219

9

AS they rode slowly into Waco, Mary knew that Clay had summarised the situation accurately. As soon as Rolf knew that Hoot and Clay were still alive — and the word would soon come to the boss — Rolf would know that his reckless living had got him into a precarious situation. It might not worry him unduly as long as he evaded capture. Being on the run was something he sneered at. It seemed he hated being tied to the ranch, and there were hideouts in Pueblo. The same situation would envelop Fogel — but maybe that gunny had been in this setup more than once. After all, his history was an unknown factor.

Clay was too tired for more conjecture, his strength ebbing with every dusty hot mile, but eventually the party entered Waco. Hoot was put to bed in his room and Doc Hawton summoned. Mary stayed by Clay and he, too, had to rest, a nice white bandage around his head, put there skilfully by the doctor.

Resting wasn't Clay's idea of doing things. But he had to while Mary and the doc were around. "How about Hoot," he asked the doc.

"He'll live, but he won't be on horseflesh for some weeks."

The news went around the town pretty swiftly. It was soon known, through O'Rourke, that Rolf Lester and Bert Fogel, along with a guy called Clip, and another unknown, were responsible for the shooting and raid on the mining camp.

When it was evident that Clay was going to be all right, Mary insisted upon riding back to her ranch. She went alone; a dangerous thing, Clay thought. But she wanted to get back to the place that was, after all, her home. Cattle and the ranch needed her.

"You will have to stay in Waco,

Clay," she commented. "Your job is here — more so with Hoot out of action."

Regretfully, he watched her go until she was just a dot on the landscape. There were so many things he wanted to ask her but it was still the wrong time. So Clay returned to his desk, despite Doc Hawton's warning that he would have a mighty sick head if he did not rest. Clay grinned faintly, thinking he'd had sick heads before today. He went out into the dusty street, restless. He called at the Last Chance. Only one bartender was serving and of Fogel there was no sign. That figured, Clay thought.

Idly, he went on to Malcolm Starn's freight-line office, as the sun began to decline. A wagon was outside and packers were working. Clay walked in. "How's the arm today?" he asked.

Starn looked up. "Fair enough, Mandell. And you?"

"Same. Listen, Bert Fogel has been gun-toting again, as you'll have heard.

How come you hired him?"

"I wanted a strong man."

"But that galoot just comes an' goes. He ain't never in the saloon. You ain't telling me the truth, Mister Starn. Now let me put you in the picture." He gave him the events in a few clipped sentences. Then: "Have you been here most of this day, Starn?"

"Sure. Check with my men — we've had a busy day."

"An' sure as hell so have I," said Clay wearily. "All right. You ain't the boss who hires Rolf Lester an' Fogel and other damned ruffians."

"Did you think I was that man?"

"Not exactly. But you acted strangely. Suppose you tell me how you got that wrist shot the same night the train was about to be derailed?"

Starn hesitated. Then: "I was down at the railroad when the posse shot up the bandits. I wanted to kill the boss."

"Who is this boss? And how come you figured to kill him?"

223

"The boss is Dave Lansing. I've been wanting him dead for a long time. Fogel gave me a hint that something was brewing that night and I kept a tag on Lansing. I thought I might be able to kill him during the raid on the train when lead would be kinda flying around. The posse started shooting instead. I was in that defile. I couldn't get a bead on Lansing, and then I got hit by a bullet. God knows who shot me. I had to ride back."

"Why did you want to kill Lansing?"

"That guy knew me long ago afore either of us ever hit Waco," said Malcolm Starn bitterly. "I'm a wanted man, Mandell. There's a sheriff in Tucson who wants me for a killing. It's a long yarn — and the hell with the details — but it was self-defence. I've been in Waco a long time now and never packed a gun. I've built up a business. Lansing kinda blackmailed me into hiring Fogel. I've been paying that feller money long enough. I guess

Lansing thought Fogel could figure out some dandy alibis if he was fixed up in the saloon, meeting men and talking without suspicion. A handy setup. That's why I had to hire Fogel."

"You can tell me, while you're being talkative, why you rode to Pueblo to meet up with Seth Mundy, Rolf Lester and Fogel."

"Wal, I just guessed Fogel would make for Pueblo. Soon as I heard there'd been a robbery at the gold company, I knew that skunk would be behind it."

"What did you reckon to do?"

Starn stared with bitter eyes out of his office window. "I thought I'd get a gun on that man when he was over the border. Killing ain't of no account in Pueblo, as you know. No sheriff or law of any kind. But the idea was a non-starter."

"Wal, Fogel ain't coming back to Waco, that's for sure," said Clay. "And maybe it won't be long before we hog-tie Lansing. Quit worrying about that sheriff in Tucson. I got no wanted posters."

Clay left, cancelling Starn from his suspicions. Tired as a broken bronc, he knew he should rest but something impelled him on. He went into the Bonanza Saloon, mixed with the ranchers, waddies and gamblers. Then Clay became aware that Lansing was watching him, smiling, unperturbed, completely in control, a remarkable man in the circumstances. "Just got back?" Clay asked grimly.

"As a matter of fact, sure, Deputy. I've been over to Pueblo."

"Sure it wasn't Monument Valley?"

Dave Lansing smoothed his black suit. Obviously he had changed his gear and was a confident man. "No, Deputy. I said Pueblo. I've been seeing pals. They'll tell you that, if you're interested. What's all this about Monument Valley?"

"Quit tryin' to fool me!" rapped Clay.

There was nothing he could extract

from this carefully-controlled man. Clay knew, of course, that there were buyers in Pueblo who would take gold and no questions asked if the price was right. Had Rolf, Fogel and the man named Clip got to the border town? It seemed likely. He also knew the town was not in his jurisdiction but that wasn't going to stop him from further action, if needed.

But all this action would have to wait for another day. He was not fool enough to wear himself to a thin wedge. He was terribly tired, weak in fact, and needed rest. His head throbbed and he needed hot food.

So early the next morning, at sunup, he rose from his bed and began preparations by washing in a tub of cold water followed by a shave with a long-handled razor. He trimmed his hair with the same blade and then went out to the Chinese eating-place for food, steak and beans for breakfast. He began to feel better.

He went to see Hoot Sampson.

"How do you feel, old-timer?"

"Not as old as all that, young feller! And I aim to get the galoots who shot me."

"Maybe I'll get them first," chuckled Clay and then he left.

He did not say anything of his plans but went to the livery and attended to a fresh horse. The bay had had enough riding recently and there were other animals in the stable.

Some time later, clad in a fresh shirt and a new hat, his gun oiled and checked, a water bottle on the saddle horn, he headed for the ramshackle town of Pueblo. As the miles went under the swiftly-moving animal, the yellow grasslands were left behind and the parched lands with the scent of sage were all around him. And in due course, dusty again, the animal sweat-flecked, he came towards the owl-hoot town and its curious mixture of inhabitants. It was now midday but apparently not too early for some galoots to patronise the cantina. He hitched his horse to a tie-rail where it would not be conspicuous among some others. He wandered along, hat down, his deputy's badge hidden, wondering just what event might come his way. Maybe he was wasting his time!

But there was a chance that Rolf, Fogel and the man named Clip were lying low in this nest of law-breakers. In fact, this was the ideal place for the men.

His face hidden, Clay watched as a few vaqueros rode in through the straggly main stem, where dust rose with every footstep or hoof. The men were all Mex in steeple-shaped hats and shapeless tilmas. He heard the greetings in Spanish. Then Clay figured it was time to enter the cantina, through the batwing doors.

Inside the place a few men leaned against the pine counter and stood in groups. At a few tables some men gambled with bored looks at desultory card games. Maybe at night the scene would be different. There were two

Mexicans who carried only knives and a 'breed with a heavy Colt. Then suddenly Clay saw Clip edge away from the bar at the far end of the room as if he had suddenly discovered there was small-pox around!

Clay smiled, noting the drunken grin had gone from the man's face, so quickly it was almost comical. He watched the man slip to a side door, stopping only to down his drink. It was this stop that enabled Clay to catch up. He went to the door in double-quick time.

Then Clay found himself in a smelly alley behind the cantina where there was nothing but alkali dust and the outline of shacks ahead. He cursed, feeling he had let the man slip. This was the rannigan who had helped Fogel and Rolf Lester in their lawless raids.

Then to his right he saw a moving man, trying to leap away from some danger. Clay knew he was the danger and he shot with equal speed after the man. But the guy had a gun.

Clay saw the belching red flame and felt the rush of the bullet past his face. Another near one! He'd have to exercise caution. As it was the man's gun had roared once and missed — and then Clay was on him. He gripped the guy by the wrist and forced the gun up. Once more the trigger squeezed but the flame and slug spat skywards. Then a savage jerk nearly broke the man's wrist and the gun dropped to the ground.

With his other hand, Clay pinned his shoulders against the wall. The man tried to hack out with his boots. Clay brought his hand away from the fellow's wrist and rammed it into his stubbly chin. He did this three times, without mercy, hurting the ruffian, making him pant and spit obscenely.

"You're the bastard who raided the mining camp! You an' Rolf an' Fogel! Where are those galoots right now? Talk!"

"You can go to hell, badge-toter!"

"I reckon you know where those gents are hiding," snarled Clay. "Talk!"

He slammed his fist repeatedly into the man's mouth, a messy business that pumped saliva and blood. The man began to groan. Clay eased off, gave the lawless galoot time to speak.

"Rolf Lester an' Fogel are at the Circle Four right now, blast you. Iffen I had my gun, I'd kill you!"

Clay released him. He did not realise he was making a mistake. Without warning, a second after Clay's grasp came away, the man doubled up sharply. He seemed to bend down and ram his fingers into his riding boots. In the next flashing moment there was a gleam of steel, jerked up as the man brought his hand up from his boot. The man had a long-bladed knife.

Clay threw back as the blade swung up in a movement that should have disembowelled him. Even so the blade ripped his shirt. As the man's arm continued its momentum, Clay moved in closer again and gripped the guy's wrist. The knife was forced above the man's head. Relentlessly, Clay forced the man's arm back and even further back. Suddenly the man named Clip cried hoarsely as his arm seemed to reach breaking point. The knife fell from his nerveless grip.

He stepped back, angry and grim. This man was a murderer. Maybe he deserved to die. Clay's fists shot out. He planted two — a right and then a left that snapped the man's head back almost to breaking his neck. The lawless man stumbled back, boots digging in the dusty ground. Suddenly he fell backwards under the impact of the driving blows and lay still. Quite still.

Breathing hard, Clay bent down to haul the man to his feet and it was then that he saw the knife rammed into an acute angle into the ruffian's back. He stared into the contorted face and knew the man was dead. Blood seeped into his clothes. The man had fallen on his own knife.

Clay dropped the body. "I'm on my way! One less — that's all!"

He moved stiffly to the front of the cantina. He unhitched his horse from the tie-rail, thinking the fracas had not attracted any attention, which was okay. He could not forget he was the deputy sheriff of Waco and as such could not play the lone game much further. If Rolf Lester had taken Fogel to the Circle Four under the impression he could fool around there in safety, Clay knew it was his duty to get a posse and go after the men. He owed it to his job, to Waco and to Hoot Sampson. A posse was the one sure way to do the job where a lone man might fail — and pay with his life!

He did not spare his animal as he thundered back to town. He could get a fresh mount later on, when he would ride out to the Circle Four with a posse. The sure-footed cayuse covered the miles, down into the browned grasslands near Waco and he rode the panting animal to the limit, then tore into Waco and threw himself off the saddle at the sheriff's office. He led the horse into the livery and, as luck would have it, the old wrangler was there. He promised to have a fresh mount ready when Clay returned.

Clay went to a saloon where he knew three rough-and-ready waddies of his acquaintance would be. They nodded at his request. They were ready to ride as sworn-in deputies. Quietly, they left with Clay, going for horses, one a big black and the other two muscled roans. There was another saloon nearby, much used by the better type of rancher, and as it happened two of Clay's pals were there and ready to ride when they heard a swift account of events.

Clay had worked as swiftly as possible. The men gathered outside the sheriff's office and were sworn in; a gabble of words, true, but sufficient! Hoot Sampson was sleeping, having been given a draught by Doc Hawton, so he did not bother him. Eventually the possemen rode out of town without any noise that would attract undue attention. In truth, the town was full of its own bustling activity. The posse settled down to a full lope that the horses could maintain for a long time.

Clay rode close to Jesse Teed, the rancher. He had not seen the cool-headed man since the time Rolf Lester had attempted to stamp on his gun-hand and Jesse had intervened. Now he gave the man the facts of the situation.

"I want those hombres brought in for trial, Jesse. I want them to start spillin' the beans about each other. Hoot and me have got evidence stacked against Fogel. I've got two of his guns. Guess he didn't waste much time getting hold of new smokepoles. The man I really want is the boss. I figure he is Dave Lansing but proving that detail might not be so easy."

He gave Jesse Teed much more information during the ride, feeling he'd be an ally on the side of law and order in the future. Then, as the hoofs covered the miles, the mesquite-covered valley that housed the Circle

Four ranch came into sight. There it lay, distant buildings in a silent and almost empty land.

All the possemen were armed but grim as they were they hoped they would not need to use weapons.

When they were close to the ranch-house and the yard, they separated and slowly nosed the horses past the corral. Clay, Jesse and another rancher walked the last few yards with measured tread right up to the ranch-house porch. Clay put his hand on the door and found it was locked. Then he noticed the windows were shuttered. He hammered grimly on the door.

"Open up! It's the law!"

10

THERE was an appreciable pause and then the ranch-house door opened slowly and framed in the doorway was Mary Lester, her eyes wide with fear, her lips parted in a swift intake of breath. Clay stared, wishing he could put his arms around her. All he said was: "Howdy, Mary. We've come for Rolf and Fogel."

"They're not here."

There seemed no sensible answer to that and with a set face he said: "Reckon we'll come in, Mary."

He stepped forward and her intake of breath became a sob. At the same moment a man stepped lithely from behind her, gun in hand, which he thrust cruelly into her back. "Don't move, Mandell — don't do anythin' you'll regret."

Rolf Lester's face was contorted with

fury as he held the gun in his sister's back. His eyes glinted pure hell and hate as they met Clay's stare. "Don't you make a move for that hogleg of yourn," he rasped, stress making him edgy. "You don't want Mary to get harmed!"

Cold anger welled-up in Clay. He had met reckless men but this was hell-bent, in-bitten badness.

"You're mad! You wouldn't kill your own sister. Put that gun away, man, and come quietly. I got a posse around the house."

"Don't push me, Mandell! You ain't foolin' me. You aim to get us to a hangnoose. Just don't try anything. You can start by moving backwards. Bert an me are coming out."

"You won't get away with this. Quit now, before Mary is hurt."

"Back off, Deputy! I hate your guts! I could easily kill you any time — an' I will! Nothing is gonna stop me gettin' out of here, nothing! You don't want Mary hurt but by God I'll use this gun on her if you don't drop back! Now move it!"

The young hell-bent's words dripped with venom, sure evidence he was ready for any shocking violence — and killing the deputy would be as nothing. Clay swallowed to ease the tightness in his throat. His head began to ache again, the bandage irksome. Clay looked at the girl, saw the awful fear in her eyes: fear of her own brother. She could hardly speak but she stammered: "Drop back Clay. He's dangerous. He'll shoot! Once he beat me! I never told you that!"

Clay had to edge backwards, his gun sweating in his palm. Jesse Teed took the hint from Clay and, with the other rancher, they stood to one side. Rolf eased out slowly, with one hand gripping Mary's shoulder, his fingers dug deep into her shirt. She was dressed for riding. Rolf's gun ground into her back and behind them appeared Bert Fogel. His Colts were on display and his eyes were alight with dangerous glints. Rolf and Fogel; mad, dangerous opponents!

Rolf Lester eased out slowly, with one hand now tightly gripping Mary's wrist. "You can back away," he hissed to Clay. "No tricks! Get back — and remember, Mandell, I ain't fooling. One wrong move and Mary will be hurt!"

There was no doubting the young buckeroo's savageness. Clay tried to think furiously. Maybe they could take chances, but Colt lead could move quicker than men — and sure as all hell Mary would get hurt! He couldn't take the chance.

Reluctantly, Clay and the other two possemen backed down, away into the ranch-yard. The other members of the posse were on the other side of the ranch-house, sent there to scout around, and they did not know what was going on.

Slowly, breathing like a man under strain, Rolf Lester edged across the yard, right behind the girl, and Fogel

241

moved so close to his partner they were as one. Rolf Lester was moving to the barn. Jesse Teed burst out "Goshdarn it! We can't let them get away!"

For every yard Rolf Lester took to the barn, accompanied by the helplessly twisting girl and Fogel, the possemen moved an equal yard. They kept in front of the vicious men. And Clay noted the tethered horses near the barn and knew the plan the lawless hombres had in mind. Three horses stood quietly, saddled, and one he felt sure had large saddle bags for a certain reason. It suddenly struck him: Rolf and Fogel had visited the Circle Four to take away some valuables. Maybe gold. Or stolen money? Or both?

The stalemate had not changed when Rolf Lester reached a horse and with a quick movement hoisted the girl onto one and lithely got up behind her, the gun still rammed into her back. With a quick leap Bert Fogel hit saddle leather, too.

Rolf Lester's voice jarred. He was

bull-tough but even his nerve had been tested by events and his comments were raspingly hoarse. Get back, Mandell! We're a-goin'! Start shooting an' Mary might be the one to get hit. Remember that!"

"Play it smart," advised Fogel, equally nervy.

At that moment they fed spurs to the horses and with a fast leap the animals went into stride. They were in such a hurry they could not get a lead rope on the third horse and the animal was left behind. But they were away, with the girl and the saddle bags packed with loot!

Rolf Lester and Fogel raced out of the ranch yard while Clay, Jesse Teed and the other rancher justifiably hesitated. Then, stung to anger, Jesse Teed threw hot lead at Fogel, regardless of the risk, perhaps without thought, and Clay heard an exclamation of pain and knew the man had been hit. But he stuck to saddle leather and rode at pell-mell lope after Rolf Lester.

The possemen ran forward, one man swearing at the way they'd been outwitted. "Tarnation! We've been done nice!" howled Jesse Teed. And then as they made for their bunched horses just outside the ranch-yard, they heard a rataplan of Colt fire. This was followed by the shrill whinnies of spooked animals and then the drum of hoofs as the scared animals raced madly away.

Rolf Lester was smart. He had stampeded the posse's horses!

"Goldarn it!" yelled a man. "That crittur of mine will run ten miles when it's spooked!"

High-heel riding boots pounded earth as the men ran for the animals, but the horses had gone, moving faster than a man, frightened by the suddenly roaring guns. And the horizon was suddenly swallowing Rolf Lester, despite the double load, and Bert Fogel. Then Clay turned back, the only one in the posse to realise one detail.

His vest flapping as he ran, he went

speedily to the barn and found the animal laden with the saddle bags jogging in a circle, bewildered by the sudden noise. Grabbing the leathers, he calmed the animal, got to the saddle and rode out of the ranch-yard, turning through the open gates so sharply the horse was nearly on its haunches. As Clay went through the running possemen, he bawled out to them: "I'm a-goin' after them galoots! You can round up your critturs! I got no time for it."

There was nothing but implacable anger in his heart for Rolf Lester, a man who would stop at nothing, risking Mary's life to save his own hide. Rolf Lester was one man in the world he could hate wholeheartedly. The man was a total villain.

Clay rowelled the horse on, but it was not a fast mover and the pack bags hampered it and the animal could not get up any speed. The fugitives had already vanished in the folds of the land, some low hills providing cover.

But as the ground began to rise he suddenly saw the shapes of rider and horse, now surprisingly far ahead. Then he lost the track and couldn't be sure which way they were going. The horse under him slowed, with no zest for reckless galloping. Well, it had been selected as a pack animal.

Clay urged the horse up to a ridge, stared ahead but there was no sign of the men ahead. Maybe they were in some shallow ravine. He reined the horse, jumped down and placed his ear to the ground and listened intently for the slightest sound radiating through the earth. It was an old Indian trick. But this little gimmick needed practice and perception to discover from any faint sound or vibration the direction of these tiny sounds. He was losing time. And he was not as wise as the old Indians. He got to the saddle again and urged the reluctant animal onwards.

He figured that if he was hampered by the saddle-bags, Rolf Lester was equally burdened because he and Bert

Fogel had their share of bags; and of course Mary as a double burden for the horse. For himself, the ground under the animal's hoofs was thin grassland, now brown with the summer sun, and the inevitable clumps of thorn bushes. This was the fringe of the Circle Four's poor quality land and maybe there were Longhorns somewhere.

Grimly, and with some satisfaction, he thought that Fogel might be having a bad time, seeing that Jesse Teed's bullet had hit him. There was no way of telling how badly he was wounded. The man had undoubtedly stuck to his saddle. The devil probably looked after his own!

He gave scant thought to the raw scar on the side of his own head. The swift events had just banished the dull headache!

He patted the saddle-bags as the horse went on at a slow lope, slowing all the time. Clay felt the animal's bony frame and thought the crittur was only good enough for pack work.

He should have forked his own horse, a better animal, but that was the trouble with swift decisions. He was stuck with it now.

The saddle-bags felt strange. This wasn't grub! He suddenly realised there were wads of U.S. dollar bills packed in the bags, loot from a raid, no doubt. And there was some weight which indicated a couple of bags of gold dust or diminutive nuggets. Well, at least he had hit the robbers where it would hurt — apart from bullet wounds in the flesh.

Clay's mount was tiring and going at a slow pace, probably the crittur's natural movement. He cursed. There was no sign of the riders ahead, indicating perhaps that they were making good use of gullies. And there was no sound of oncoming riders from the general direction of the Circle Four ranch buildings, now miles distant, which suggested the posse were badly left behind. Maybe some of the men had still not retrieved their nags!

All at once, like a savage reminder that this was a grim trail of death, he saw a motionless shape lying on the earth a few hundred yards ahead. At first he thought the shape was Fogel and that the guy had toppled from his saddle in death. But no such luck.

Then the shape moved, rolled on the ground. Clay scooped at his Colt, grim, his reactions too far ahead of thought. He did not fire his gun.

The person on the ground was a girl — Mary Lester! As he cantered the nag up to the spot he saw that her hands and legs were bound with manilla. But she wasn't gagged and managed to cry out: "Clay! Oh, God! Help me!"

She had seen his approach. As he leaped from the horse and took her in his arms, she added: "They set me down here alone! I was a nuisance! Oh, God — my own brother!"

"Mangy coyote!" Clay swore.

He took out a knife from his belt scabbard and cut swiftly through the rope. "Whose idea was it to bind you?

What iffen I never found you? This is still a big land! You'd have died."

"Oh, Clay — thank goodness it's you! Clay, hold me!"

He did just that for some valuable moments, precious time together even if the backdrop was harsh and the circumstances hardly ideal. At last Mary was his: he knew that. They didn't need words to realise they had found each other — in more ways than one.

He helped her to her feet. "We've got to ride back, Mary, slowly no doubt with this nag." He smiled. "Can't hurry the crittur!"

I know where they are going," she choked.

"Who?"

"Fogel and my awful brother. They're heading for the City of the Moon. You know the place — that old Indian stone town carved out of the rocks hundreds of years ago by the ancient tribe, but now forgotten."

How did you learn that?"

"I heard Fogel mention it. He is hit

bad and he can't ride for ever. He's got a bullet in his shoulder and it's bleeding badly. I heard him saying something about this City of the Moon. As if it might mean something."

"Maybe they figure to lie low, Mary. But damn them. You're heading back to your home. I'll get this nag ready. It can take a double load for some time, and if it tires too much I can walk with the brute."

They climbed to the horse's back and set off at a slow plodding gait. The nag did not complain and seemed to accept the slow movement and double load as part of destiny. And the animal had its own instinct for home. In this way they covered some distance while the sun passed its zenith. They did not encounter the possemen.

Mary's nearness was strangely exhilarating to Clay Mandell. He knew there was only one woman for him and that was Mary. And as for the girl, she was forgetting the lies Rolf had told her about Clay concerning Tad's death and other stupid tales. She knew that Clay was fine — and that he loved her.

A few miles from the Circle Four buildings they rode into two members of the posse who were out searching vainly for sign. They rode back to the ranch and the saddle-bags were stowed away safely. Sure enough they contained a large amount of currency and the bags of dust and gold nuggets, all stolen goods which would have to be accounted for in time and probably returned to the legal owners. But that was for the future.

Clay was careful about the saddle-bags. They would prove the case against Rolf Lester and Fogel, but what he wanted was a damning indictment against Dave Lansing, the boss man of many of these raids.

He found his own horse nosing for grass near the ranch and there was his rifle still in the saddle boot. The other men had got their animals collected again. There was still the problem of how to hunt for Rolf Lester and

Fogel. So they had a meeting and Mary made a quick meal for the men. Clay thought about Hoot Sampson back there in Waco and hoped the sheriff was progressing well.

It was decided to start out for the City of the Moon at the earliest moment of sunup the next day. They were running out of time for that day, anyway, and with Fogel wounded the men would not be making a fast getaway. The City of the Moon was obviously a place to hole up. That much was sure, but what else was in the minds of the two desperate outlaws was not quite certain.

The next day, from the Circle Four, as a base where they made plans — such as they could — and the animals were rested, guns checked and grim thoughts put to one side, the posse rode out for the old Indian town. Clay knew the desert enveloped the old city, as it had done for the past three hundred years, and the old Indian caves were mainly a home for rattlers and scorpions and little else.

He felt pretty sure they would find Rolf Lester and Fogel still in hiding, grim desperate men with little choice except hard riding in desert lands. Rolf might be able to reach safety; but what about Bert Fogel? Wounded, he was a liability!

11

WHEN Mary was finally left alone at the Circle Four she sat down and naturally fell to worried thought. She was not entirely alone. Old Tom Week was on hand in case she needed help in anything.

Still, in her thoughts she pictured the posse riding out to the old caves, known rather grandly in local myths as the City of the Moon, and her brother figured largely in her troubled mind. Why had they gone to this place? Was it just a hideout, or was there another reason? Would Rolf ever return to the ranch? She remembered the old days when he and Tad were boys, reckless even then. Something in their blood had impelled them on to a lawless life.

She wished she could stop thinking about him, even if it was the old times when he wasn't quite so hell-bent.

And then there was Clay; and she felt so anxious about him. But he would return safely — surely? As a deputy, now doing the job of sheriff in Hoot's enforced absence, there was bound to be danger.

The ranch was being neglected, she thought. She couldn't cope with all the work, and there was only Tom Week to help her. Although the spread was not a rich one, it could be improved if work was done. But now there was no one to do anything.

Restlessly she rose and picked up some needlework but her mind was not on it. Maybe she ought to get into the ranch-yard and do some other work, maybe help Tom.

A knock sounded on the outer ranch-house door. She went to the door but did not open up. She called out: "Who is it?"

"Let me in, Mary. It's Dave Lansing. Are Rolf and Fogel there?"

She did not open the door. She was

glad it was bolted from the inside. And the windows were shuttered, too. She moved grimly across the room and picked up a shotgun. Swiftly, she checked that it was loaded with two cartridges. She returned to the door. "They are not here. Please go away. You are bad news — the law wants you."

"I arranged to meet the men here; but I'm late, I guess."

"The posse are after them — as they will soon be after you."

"Is that so? Why do you talk like that to me? Where are they heading? Maybe I can do something to help Rolf, huh?"

"They've gone to the City of the Moon, if you must know."

She heard his sudden exclamations. "Those double-crossing rats! That's the game! Wal, that settles it! Those hellions won't get away from the posse. That City of the Moon — what a lousy name! — is nothing but a rat trap, an' they are the rats! But I'm going while those lawmen are out there — an damn that deputy Clay Mandell! Adios, Mary! I'm pulling up stakes, if you want to know, and lighting out for Mexico. Plenty of opportunity down by the Rio Grande for a feller like me. I've sold the Bonanza; made the deal yesterday. Rolf is a fool. Him and Fogel might get that currency we hid up there, from the bank raids and the like, but they won't get out of that trap they're in. City of the Moon — hell! A rat trap for sure. There ain't any water for miles around. The posse and that deputy will have them to rights in no time."

The man's laughter, so callous, brought a cloud of red anger into her brain. She heard him walk across the porch. He intended to escape justice while Rolf paid the penalty! Oh, the injustice of it all! She hated the man in that awful moment of red anger in her mind.

She slipped the bolts on the door. She saw his figure outside. "Dave Lansing!" she called.

He turned and saw the levelled shotgun. He tried to whip at a small gun he kept in a shoulder holster inside his jacket. The shotgun roared death. Mary staggered backwards with the kick of her gun. She suddenly felt sick at the sight of spurting blood oozing from the prone body. She knew the man was dead — and she had killed him. Oh, God what had she done! She dropped the shotgun as Tom Week came rushing out into the ranch yard. She ran into the house and bolted the door again. She sank into a seat and pressed her fingers to her temple. Feeling sick at heart she wondered how it had all happened. How could she cope with all this?

With all her yearning heart she knew she needed Clay by her side, to help and advise her: but he was not on hand. In that moment she realised she would need that guy for the rest of her life!

★ ★ ★

Clay Mandell walked slowly up the incline, rifle at the ready, hip high. His keen eyes searched the holes in the cliff face. He was watching this mystical City of the Moon for sudden movement of any figure against the yellow stone, man or horse. Somewhere in this ancient warren of crumbling caves, Rolf and Fogel must be hiding. He was still unsure about their motives. What had brought these two bad-hats across the arid lands to this silent place? Surely it wasn't just because they could hole up. That might be important to a man who was wounded and finding travel difficult, but Rolf was surely fit enough. If they pressed on, they could have reached Mexico without much more effort.

The remainder of the posse was moving slowly forward from different directions, keeping under cover behind rocks as much as possible, guns in hand. "I'll give 'em a shout," Clay called to Jesse Teed. He raised his voice. "Hello, there!"

The echoes came back at him. Then there was silence. Clay tried again. "We're a-coming for you, Lester! Come on out, hands up. You, too, Fogel!"

But only silence reigned after the echoes died away. There was no movement, no sign of man or beast. If they were there, they were well hidden.

"Maybe they've got out — ridden on," said Jesse Teed.

Then from somewhere inside a cave a shot rang out. A second later another Colt barked inside the ancient holes, and as the sounds died away the possemen glanced at each other, for no bullets had sliced their way and they'd seen no gunflashes.

"Them fellers are fightin' among themselves," shouted Jesse Teed.

Clay nodded. "Seems like it. Well, when rogues fall out, honest men come into their own!"

Inside the cave Rolf and Fogel had found the hidden loot. The greater portion of the currency had been Dave

Lansing's, bills that were too hot to handle. It had been Lansing's idea to cache them in this old Indian site for the simple reason that no one ever came this way. Indians avoided it and there was nothing but sand and rock for prospectors. Later, when conditions were right, Lansing planned to circulate the money, spend it on various projects and pay his underlings. He had confided in Rolf Lester, and Rolf had talked with Fogel. Now they had the loot.

They lifted stones from a hidden cavity and withdrew the wads of money. This was bank money. Fogel's eyes glinted with greed — and pain. Rolf eyed him grimly. "There's a cave that runs right back through the hill from here. Kinda tunnel. But you can't get a hoss through. Some places the tunnel roof is only three feet high."

They had divided the loot roughly. And there was more on the two horses, tied around the saddle horns.

"What'll we do on the other side

without hosses?" snarled Fogel.

"Walk. We can't use the animals."

"I can't walk far — you know that. Ain't it desert on the other side of this hill?"

"Yep. Nine miles on there's an Indian encampment. They've got cayuses."

"Nine miles of desert — an no water! We'll never make it."

"You won't make it," agreed Rolf Lester.

Rage tinged Fogel's cheeks. He made to pick up some of the currency, a wad lying near to him, but with all the old instincts of a gunman flaring in a sudden rage, his good hand whipped to his gun instead. He scooped it out of leather and triggered the weapon.

But Rolf Lester had seen the play coming and his gun was in his grip and it fired simultaneously with Fogel's. Rolf Lester felt a slug bite searingly into his flesh, the impact making him stagger back until he tripped.

When he got to his feet, swearing viciously, Fogel was undoubtedly dead.

There was a jagged hole in his head out of which blood bubbled sickeningly. "The hell with you, bastard!" Rolf swore.

Strangely, the slug he fancied had hit into his flesh did not hurt — and there was a good satisfying reason. Rolf took out a thick wad of dollar notes from inside his shirt and looked at them. The slug from Fogel's gun was embedded in the wad. That had made the impact that had made him stagger.

He'd been lucky. He felt triumphant, taking it as a symbol of his everlasting luck. He would get through to the Indian camp, get a pony from them. He'd be all right! Rolf grinned again. He was not going the way of Fogel. He could cross the desert on the other side of the hill when he got through the low-roofed tunnel.

He began to pack as much money and a bag of gold dust as he could carry. He hid the rest of the loot under a rock, figuring he'd be back some day for the small fortune. Finally he was ready to leave. He had two Colts with him, one in his holster and the other stuck in his belt. His horse was ground-hitched just out of sight and he would have to go on without the animal because of the low-roofed tunnel behind him. He had scouted this tunnel previously and he congratulated himself on that point.

★ ★ ★

Clay Mandell had shrewdly estimated the location of the shots which the posse had heard. He was the first to run forward, walking more carefully as he approached the cave mouth. He sidled along, peered into the first few yards of the silent place and wondered grimly if a gun would roar at him. He turned into the rocky, jagged mouth, saw the horses and noted the wanted men had left their rifles in the saddle boots. He went deeply into the cave, his eyes accustomed to the light that filtered through cracks in the roof. A rustle prompted him to raise his Colt swiftly. Looking up, he saw three black vultures perched high in the rock. Birds of ill omen! But they didn't carry guns. He went on and behind him came Jesse Teed and two possemen. They came to the chamber where Bert Fogel lay dead.

"Sure figured they were fightin'," muttered Jesse Teed.

"And this is what they were fighting about," declared Clay, and he held up the wad of bank currency and looked curiously at the embedded slug.

"Someone has had hell's luck," said Jesse Teed.

"Rolf," said Clay.

Clay moved down the cave, realising that Rolf Lester had found a way of escape. He had killed Fogel and left the horses. Clay went ahead with more speed although the cave floor was littered with fallen rock. Evidently the cave roof had a tendency to crumble. In fact, it was dangerous.

Clay was ahead of the others. All at once he heard the distant scrape of boots on rock and guessed it was Rolf Lester making good his escape. Clay rounded a boulder, crouching now that the roof was lower.

Rolf Lester heard the sounds of pursuit. Angrily, he snapped off three shots into the half-light behind him in the faint hope he would target some moving person.

Clay felt the rush of slugs around his head and he, too, whipped off two answering shots from his own gun.

It was a fatal thing to do. With horrible suddenness there came the ominous rumble of crashing rock just ahead in the tunnel. He heard a shrill wild scream and then more awful rumbling as rock came down. Clay flinched back, his mouth full of dust, staggering, shielding his head. He knew he had to get back down the tunnel.

The vibrations from the rataplan of sudden shots had brought the loose roof down. The noise was pretty frightening and he knew that Rolf Lester had not escaped this time. Clay staggered back to Jesse Teed and the other men, his mouth full of dust, but that did not stop him saying: "He's dead — an' buried!"

★ ★ ★

They rode back across the semi-arid lands almost immediately, taking as evidence the wad of money with the embedded slug and the two horses they'd found at the cave mouth. There were saddle bags still on these horses.

Clay began to smile tiredly. Once more he was riding into Waco with bad news, at least for Mary. Once more he was leaving a dead Lester back in the waste-lands. But he was sure this time the girl would understand and accept. She would listen to him, and he'd help her forget her hell-bent brothers.

He looked at the setting sun and thought surely Waco would provide him with a rest. He had done his job. And there'd be another day. There was always another day with those who had faith: and he had faith there'd be a future with Mary.

He began to grin. "Say, Jesse — I figure I'm heading for a wedding pretty soon!"

The other man smiled back. "Wal, after all this I hope I'm a special guest! Let's get to town, Clay, and have a drink!"

THE END

TOP HAND
Wade Everett

The Broken T was big. But no ranch is big enough to let a man hide from himself.

GUN WOLVES OF LOBO BASIN
Lee Floren

The Feud was a blood debt. When Smoke Talbot found the outlaws who gunned down his folks he aimed to nail their hide to the barn door.

SHOTGUN SHARKEY
Marshall Grover

The westbound coach carrying the indomitable Larry and Stretch headed for a shooting showdown.

FIGHTING RAMROD
Charles N. Heckelmann

Most men would have cut their losses, but Frazer counted the bullets in his guns and said he'd soak the range in blood before he'd give up another inch of what was his.

LONE GUN
Eric Allen

Smoke Blackbird had been away too long. The Lequires had seized the Blackbird farm, forcing the Indians and settlers off, and no one seemed willing to fight! He had to fight alone.

THE THIRD RIDER
Barry Cord

Mel Rawlins wasn't going to let anything stand in his way. His father was murdered, his two brothers gone. Now Mel rode for vengeance.

ARIZONA DRIFTERS
W. C. Tuttle

When drifting Dutton and Lonnie Steelman decide to become partners they find that they have a common enemy in the formidable Thurston brothers.

TOMBSTONE
Matt Braun

Wells Fargo paid Luke Starbuck to outgun the silver-thieving stagecoach gang at Tombstone. Before long Luke can see the only thing bearing fruit in this eldorado will be the gallows tree.

HIGH BORDER RIDERS
Lee Floren

Buckshot McKee and Tortilla Joe cut the trail of a border tough who was running Mexican beef into Texas. They stopped the smuggler in his tracks.

BRETT RANDALL, GAMBLER
E. B. Mann

Larry Day had the choice of running away from the law or of assuming a dead man's place. No matter what he decided he was bound to end up dead.

THE GUNSHARP
William R. Cox

The Eggerleys weren't very smart. They trained their sights on Will Carney and Arizona's biggest blood bath began.

THE DEPUTY OF SAN RIANO
Lawrence A. Keating and
Al. P. Nelson

When a man fell dead from his horse, Ed Grant was spotted riding away from the scene. The deputy sheriff rode out after him and came up against everything from gunfire to dynamite.

FARGO: MASSACRE RIVER
John Benteen

The ambushers up ahead had now blocked the road. Fargo's convoy was a jumble, a perfect target for the insurgents' weapons!

SUNDANCE: DEATH IN THE LAVA
John Benteen

The Modoc's captured the wagon train and its cargo of gold. But now the halfbreed they called Sundance was going after it . . .

HARSH RECKONING
Phil Ketchum

Five years of keeping himself alive in a brutal prison had made Brand tough and careless about who he gunned down . . .

FARGO: PANAMA GOLD
John Benteen

With foreign money behind him, Buckner was going to destroy the Panama Canal before it could be completed. Fargo's job was to stop Buckner.

FARGO:
THE SHARPSHOOTERS
John Benteen

The Canfield clan, thirty strong were raising hell in Texas. Fargo was tough enough to hold his own against the whole clan.

PISTOL LAW
Paul Evan Lehman

Lance Jones came back to Mustang for just one thing — revenge! Revenge on the people who had him thrown in jail.

HELL RIDERS
Steve Mensing

Wade Walker's kid brother, Duane, was locked up in the Silver City jail facing a rope at dawn. Wade was a ruthless outlaw, but he was smart, and he had vowed to have his brother out of jail before morning!

DESERT OF THE DAMNED
Nelson Nye

The law was after him for the murder of a marshal — a murder he didn't commit. Breen was after him for revenge — and Breen wouldn't stop at anything . . . blackmail, a frameup . . . or murder.

DAY OF THE COMANCHEROS
Steven C. Lawrence

Their very name struck terror into men's hearts — the Comancheros, a savage army of cutthroats who swept across Texas, leaving behind a bloodstained trail of robbery and murder.

SUNDANCE: SILENT ENEMY
John Benteen

A lone crazed Cheyenne was on a personal war path. They needed to pit one man against one crazed Indian. That man was Sundance.

LASSITER
Jack Slade

Lassiter wasn't the kind of man to listen to reason. Cross him once and he'll hold a grudge for years to come — if he let you live that long.

LAST STAGE TO GOMORRAH
Barry Cord

Jeff Carter, tough ex-riverboat gambler, now had himself a horse ranch that kept him free from gunfights and card games. Until Sturvesant of Wells Fargo showed up.

McALLISTER ON THE COMANCHE CROSSING
Matt Chisholm

The Comanche, McAllister owes them a life — and the trail is soaked with the blood of the men who had tried to outrun them before.

QUICK-TRIGGER COUNTRY
Clem Colt

Turkey Red hooked up with Curly Bill Graham's outlaw crew. But wholesale murder was out of Turk's line, so when range war flared he bucked the whole border gang alone . . .

CAMPAIGNING
Jim Miller

Ambushed on the Santa Fe trail, Sean Callahan is saved by two Indian strangers. But there'll be more lead and arrows flying before the band join Kit Carson against the Comanches.

GUNSLINGER'S RANGE
Jackson Cole

Three escaped convicts are out for revenge. They won't rest until they put a bullet through the head of the dirty snake who locked them behind bars.

RUSTLER'S TRAIL
Lee Floren

Jim Carlin knew he would have to stand up and fight because he had staked his claim right in the middle of Big Ike Outland's best grass.

THE TRUTH ABOUT SNAKE RIDGE
Marshall Grover

The troubleshooters came to San Cristobal to help the needy. For Larry and Stretch the turmoil began with a brawl and then an ambush.

WOLF DOG RANGE
Lee Floren

Will Ardery would stop at nothing, unless something stopped him first — like a bullet from Pete Manly's gun.

DEVIL'S DINERO
Marshall Grover

Plagued by remorse, a rich old reprobate hired the Texas Troubleshooters to deliver a fortune in greenbacks to each of his victims.

GUNS OF FURY
Ernest Haycox

Dane Starr, alias Dan Smith, wanted to close the door on his past and hang up his guns, but people wouldn't let him.

DONOVAN
Elmer Kelton

Donovan was supposed to be dead. Uncle Joe Vickers had fired off both barrels of a shotgun into the vicious outlaw's face as he was escaping from jail. Now Uncle Joe had been shot — in just the same way.

CODE OF THE GUN
Gordon D. Shirreffs

MacLean came riding home, with saddle tramp written all over him, but sewn in his shirt-lining was an Arizona Ranger's star.

GAMBLER'S GUN LUCK
Brett Austen

Gamblers seldom live long. Parker was a hell of a gambler. It was his life — or his death . . .

ORPHAN'S PREFERRED
Jim Miller

Sean Callahan answers the call of the Pony Express and fights Indians and outlaws to get the mail through.

DAY OF THE BUZZARD
T. V. Olsen

All Val Penmark cared about was getting the men who killed his wife.

THE MANHUNTER
Gordon D. Shirreffs

Lee Kershaw knew that every Rurale in the territory was on the lookout for him. But the offer of $5,000 in gold to find five small pieces of leather was too good to turn down.